Eradicated

Book Five
Duty and Deception Series

By
JL Redington

© JL Redington 2015

No part of this publication may be reproduced, or stored in a retrieval system, or transmitted in any form or by any means, electronic, mechanical, photocopying, recording or otherwise without written permission of the author.

Table of Contents

Prologue
Chapter One
Chapter Two
Chapter Three
Chapter Four
Chapter Five
Chapter Six
Chapter Seven
Chapter Eight
Chapter Nine
Chapter Ten
Chapter Eleven
Chapter Twelve
Epilogue

Prologue

Tristan Bradford lay in a luxurious four-post king bed with a heavy gold and black comforter over him. He was surrounded by things beyond elegant and well into decadent. As he gazed slowly around the incredible room, he wondered if he would want to live in this hotel and rent a suite on the top floor. Why not? He'd worked hard, hadn't he? It was time to sit back and enjoy the nice things this world had to offer.

That said, Bradford began to feel that old familiar itch that could never be scratched. His mind returned to that gold mine of an algorithm inside Neo Weston's head. Right now he could actually see what he could do with that kind of money. The craving inside him to have that money in his accounts made his brain spin with plans and ideas and…oh so much more.

It was midnight in Toulouse, Italy, and he needed to make a decision. Should he return to the States and get that information out of Weston's head, or should he stay safe and warm under this wonderful comforter? In the end, his addiction to the chase and the money got him up and out of bed. He went straight to the phone and booked himself on a flight to Richmond, hoping to stay out of FBI sight with his new identity.

Before he left the telephone in its cradle, however, he made one more call. He'd checked out his 'team' members and found that Raymond Mathens was on his way to Brazil at this exact time. Bradford dialed the number from his black book.

"Yes?"

"I need a job done, in the next five hours. I'll pay extra for the short notice."

Chapter One

Tristan Bradford had his arm firmly around Sophia's neck, his gun to her head. Neo pointed his gun at Bradford from fifty feet away, ready to take him out.

"Write it down. Write down the algorithm NOW and I let her live."

Neo calculated his odds, quickly and efficiently. Sophia had been threatening premature labor for nearly a week. If he were to shoot Bradford, he could scare Sophia into labor and the baby was a good nine weeks from their delivery date. If he didn't shoot, would Bradford really let her live? Bradford only wanted the algorithm for his own greedy purposes. For Neo, it was never about the money, it was always about making it available to everyone. He'd never written the code down before, but now he had no choice.

Raising his gun over his head, he motioned with the other hand that he was reaching into the vest pocket of his body armor.

"I'm getting my notepad and pen. Don't shoot. I'm going to write it down."

Neo set his weapon on the ground and scrawled the information on the notepad. "See? Here it is. It's on the pad, now let her go." He tore the paper from the pad. "It's yours, as soon as you let her go."

Bradford released his terrified prisoner and she ran toward Neo. Suddenly, a shot rang out and Sophia's face changed from terror to sorrow. Her hand reached instantly to her belly and she staggered forward and fell to the ground.

"NOOOO!" Neo grabbed his gun from the ground beside him and ran to her, falling to his knees as another shot rang out. He felt the bullet enter just inside the armhole of his vest. As he fell to the ground he could hear an infant crying in the background and his body began moving side to side, side to side, side to side...

"Neo! Neo! You're dreaming again. *Wake up*."

Neo gasped as air rushed into his lungs. He sat straight up in bed and grabbed Sophia with both arms, holding her tightly. She stroked his back, whispering softly to him.

"It's okay, my love. It was just a dream. We're all okay." Sophia's voice was soft, gentle and reassuring. Neo could feel his body slowly relaxing.

He reached down with one arm and set his hand on her barely swollen belly. In his dream she was much further along.

Sophia stroked his face. "Was it the same nightmare?"

"Yes."

"Neo, I've never known you to have nightmares before. Even when I didn't know the work you did, you *never* had dreams like this."

"I know, I know. I'm not sure I understand it myself. But I've never had a new life involved in one of my ops before. I've always known, no matter what happens I can protect us. But this dream makes me feel powerless to protect you and the baby. And this time, I heard him cry."

"You're going to protect us all, Neo, even Mrs. Barbosa. Between you and the rest of the Bureau, this baby won't be able to fill his diaper without the whole city of Washington D.C. knowing about it."

Neo chuckled softly. The two of them snuggled down into the blankets and Sophia rested her head on his shoulder, feeling the muscles in his arms flexing and relaxing. "Showoff," she murmured. Neo chuckled.

"Just making sure you understand the incredibleness of my 'guns.'"

Sophia giggled and snuggled in closer and in minutes she was back to sleep. She never complained when he woke her up with his nightmares. She was always worried about him, never about herself. He was amazed at how open she was with her love for him, and at how easily she shared herself with him. Neo felt Sophia was everything he knew love to be. She was going to be an amazing mother.

Neo lay in bed trying not to think about the dream, but there was something about it that always drew him in. There was something he was supposed to see, but he never could figure out what it was. And so he began, like so many nights previously, picking the dream apart to try and find that one 'something' he knew he was supposed to see.

The man was definitely Tristan Bradford. He was holding his wife at gunpoint. His face was evil, twisted, shining in the moonlight. He could never see Sophia's face, but he knew the woman was his wife. The setting…maybe it was the setting.

They were in a small clearing. It must have been at a park, because the grass they stood on was cut short by a mower. Around them there were trees…no…not trees. Around them there were bushes, large, full, green bushes.

Neo's eyes were closed now as he forced himself to examine the scene around them. He couldn't let himself look at Bradford or Sophia. They were frozen in place and he was able to move around them, seeing them in three dimensions. This was new. He'd never been able to see the whole scene before in 3D. Intrigued, he continued to push himself to focus on the scene around them, not on Sophia, quashing his fear for her life. All players in the dream were frozen in place, except for Neo, and now, he could reason with himself. He explained to himself he had no need to fear for his wife because this was just a dream.

The soft moonlight shone brightly on the scene before him showing the evil shining from Bradford's eyes, the grass, the bushes, Sophia frozen in fear as the bullet pierces her back…

Neo's eyes popped open and he swallowed the gasp that threatened to wake Sophia yet again. It was dawn outside the windows and he wasn't sure if he'd slept or been asleep or awake as he walked his nightmare. Surely he couldn't have been sleeping while talking to himself like he was awake, but it seemed like hours had passed. He must have fallen asleep at some point.

Moving the blankets slowly so not to disturb Sophia, he gently lifted her hand from his chest and kissed it softly, setting it on his pillow. He walked to the long windows and moved the curtain to the side, staring out over the city. Was it smart to live in the fray? Should he have required Sophia and Mrs. Barbosa to leave and go into witness protection somewhere far away? No one would ever have found them in their island home had he not come back to D.C. to help Desmond. He didn't regret the decision to help his friend; he only regretted revealing his family's hiding place. Now he wondered if he could truly keep them safe.

The building they lived in was now a veritable fortress, thanks to the Bureau. Entering the building required a retinal scan or fingerprint depending on the door that was entered. The only residences in the entire building were the penthouses, of which there were three. The remainder of the building was office space, which made it easier to monitor the comings and goings than it would be in a building with hundreds of apartment dwellers. The penthouses in this building were put in when it was built to house foreign guests for a high finance company that since had gone belly up. The building owners decided to rent out the large apartments on the top floor which worked out very well for Neo. The other two penthouses were vacant, and would stay that way until Bradford was found. That made guarding Neo's penthouse all the easier. Still, Bradford had somehow managed to get into the building undetected, then overcome two guards at the door and enter their unit unnoticed by either Sophia or Mrs. Barbosa. Security was much tighter in and around the building for that reason, thanks to Cayman. No such breaches had occurred since the security upgrade, and Neo felt much better about leaving his family where they were.

A shiver went down his spine and he turned to see his beautiful wife watching him.

"I thought you were asleep."

"I was, but how can I sleep when you're parading those cute buns all over the bedroom? Why waste a perfectly good view with sleep?"

She moved her hands over her head and a stretch traveled from her fingertips down her body, over her petite protruding belly and down her legs to her toes. He grinned watching her.

"That looked like it felt good."

"Mmmm," she said patting the empty place beside her. "Come back to bed and snuggle me."

"You read my mind. Besides, my cute buns are cold." He pranced backwards, displaying his backside for Sophia to see. She laughed as he plopped down on the bed and cuddled in beside her.

"This is my favorite part of the day," she said, getting as close to him as she could.

"Oh, I don't know. I rather like riding in the SUV with Cayman."

Sophia jerked her head back, gave him a mock angry look and slapped him playfully, then nuzzled back in. Neo checked the time. It was approaching seven a.m. Sophia moved his face away from the clock.

"No, don't look at it. Just stay here with me today. We could play Scrabble and watch Jeopardy. I'm so much better at Jeopardy than you are, and I could show off my smartness."

Neo laughed. "Oh, you think so? Well I highly doubt that you're better than I am. I say you start recording them, without watching the episodes mind you, and we'll just have to have a playoff. I'll make the popcorn."

"Oh, good luck with making anything in *that* kitchen! Mrs. Barbosa will tan your hide if you try that."

"Yeah? Well I'm bigger than she is and I can shoot a gun."

"Don't get cocky. She has a broom and she knows how to use it."

Neo gazed down at the woman he loved more than anything in the entire world. How could he love a child when all the love he had was poured into this one human being? He smiled at her.

"You know, you're pretty selfish."

Sophia started laughing and spoke through her laugher. "What brought that up?"

"Well, just look at you. You're hogging all my love and I don't know if there's going to be anything left for our son. I'd say that was pretty selfish."

Sophia shook her head, her eyes glowing up at him. "You mean our daughter, of course, and just you wait. I've heard amazing things about how a parent can love."

"No, actually I mean our son, and I'll be the judge of that. I will tell you this, if it's a girl, I'm sending her back."

"You're hurting her feelings. She's crying now, ya big meanie. She thinks her daddy doesn't love her because she doesn't have a penis. How sad is *that*?"

"Oh, tell her to chill. I love you, after all and *you* don't have a penis. I've always known you were a little jealous of mine."

"And I thought I'd hid that so well." Sophia grabbed the spare pillow and began pummeling her husband with it.

"Hey! I'm just trying to be honest here."

Neo grabbed the pillow and pulled it from her hands, throwing it on the floor. He took her in his arms and lay her down on her pillow, covering her mouth with his. Every cell of her body responded to him.

They were interrupted by a knock on the door. It was Mrs. Barbosa.

"You be nice to Mrs. Neo!" she called through the door. "She a very delicate flower right now. No make me come in there!"

"Yes, Mrs. Barbosa," said Neo, stifling a laugh. "You're a 'delicate flower' now? Oh, if she only knew what you were capable of."

"Why," said Sophia breathlessly, "I have *no* idea what you're talking about. Really I don't."

Neo grabbed her and kissed her soundly. Sophia muffled a squeal; her smile prevented a solid kiss.

"Kiss me or you'll be stuck here all day."

In her best southern bell accent she said, "Oh, Mr. Neo, surely you wouldn't want to deprive this delicate flower of her nourishment? Now, would you?"

Neo released her and lay back in bed shaking his head. He rose and 'sauntered' into the bathroom. Sophia burst into laughter at his runway walk.

Chapter Two

Now walking without the aid of a cane, Desmond stood in the firing range with the rifle to his shoulder, the cane leaning against the shelf in front of him. He'd already practiced with a pistol and was now listening to his instructor as he adjusted Desmond's stance, moved his feet and positioned his hands on the rifle and the rifle on his shoulder.

Over the last several weeks, as Desmond's wounds healed, he realized he needed to hone his shooting skills. He wasn't looking to become an expert marksman, but he did want to make sure if he needed to, he could shoot a gun accurately and safely. As a research physician, he had little to no need, or opportunity, to fire a gun. The situation with Neo made him realize he'd gone into a very dangerous situation without a way to defend himself. He wasn't going to let that *ever* happen again.

Focusing now on where he wanted the bullet to go, he fixed the target in his mind and gently squeezed the trigger. The gun fired, but completely missed the target.

"How can that happen when I'm staring right at it?" Desmond wanted to throw the gun at the target, along with the bullet. The frustrations he'd dealt with after his abduction came to a head in this moment and he wanted to toss every table, pound every shooter, and yell obscenities at the top of his voice. But he didn't. He'd learned over the weeks that these feelings came up every now and again and he recognized it right away this time. To combat the angry urges, Desmond calmed himself with deep breaths, gently laying the rifle down until he regained control. He would figure out how to fire the gun. He would practice until he did. There were no time constraints to worry about…he could do this.

His instructor waited until Desmond was back in control. It took several seconds, but before long Desmond raised the rifle once again, focusing down the barrel and through the sight to the target. He squeezed the trigger once again and the bullet flew from the barrel through the center of the target.

"Great shot!" His instructor clapped Desmond on the back. "That's exactly what determination will do for you."

Desmond grinned and shook his hand. "I've got a lot of practicing ahead of me, but I think I'm getting it."

Agent Andre Wilson, one of the two day guards responsible for protecting Desmond and Ciara, drove Desmond home from the shooting range. The other guard, Agent Jay Green, was at the hotel with Ciara. During the silent ride back to the hotel where he'd been hidden away by the Bureau, Desmond had time to think. It seemed Bradford was focusing in on Neo now.

Did that mean he'd leave Desmond alone? He and Ciara were more than ready to go home, leave the hotel behind them, and have their lives back. Maybe they'd take that trip to Hawaii and get married. He just wanted a normal life again, one that didn't involve rogue operations and bad guys. He was done.

The Bureau was hesitant to allow either Desmond or Ciara back to work just yet, and Ciara was about ready to bite everyone in her field of vision, in fact, she often did. Desmond no longer needed the care she'd been so busy providing and she was bored. He'd invited her to come along and learn to shoot with him, to take lessons with him, but she wanted nothing to do with it.

Desmond had spoken with Neo a few days ago about the situation and they decided Neo would talk to Ciara's boss at the magazine. In this day of electronic everything, Desmond was certain the work she did could be done from the hotel and he thought maybe it would be enough to take her mind off being in 'lock up' as she liked to refer to their situation.

He came through the door into their suite and found Ciara with a huge smile on her face. She strode quickly across the room and threw her arms around Desmond's neck.

"Thank you for doing this," she said. "You have no idea what this means to me." She let go of him and stood before him, taking both his hands in hers. "My boss called and set me up to work from the suite. I'm just waiting for the official nod from the tech department and I'll be able to log into the network and start working again. I'm so happy!"

"What is it you said you did, again?" Desmond put on his best inquiring face.

"Oh, very funny," she said. "I just can't wait to get started!"

Desmond hugged her. "Congratulations. I'm happy they could make this happen."

"I don't know why I didn't think of doing this," she said, smiling up at him. "But this is just one of those ways I will always know you have my back, Desmond Ashler. I love you for thinking of it."

"You've done an amazing job of helping me get back on my feet. I couldn't have done it without you." Desmond kissed her and Ciara's eyes widened as she suddenly released his lips and stepped back.

"I've got so much to do! I have to get a filing system set up, get my computer files in order, my contacts all have to be informed that I'm back…I've got to get busy."

Ciara wandered off, talking to herself about the work she needed to get done. It was good to see her busy again. Desmond smiled as he watched her walk away. She was not just compassionate, but she was beautiful, smart and funny, as well. She was also incredibly organized in both her personal life and her work. She was going to be fine, and it made him smile.

There was a knock at the door, which was odd. Ciara spun around to face Desmond, a look of fear on her face. The Bureau always came through the adjoining room, knocking on that room door first. Desmond went to the door that led into the protection detail room and found Agent Winston already coming through.

"There's a guy at the door with a rolling serving tray. Did you order some lunch on your own?"

"No, we always order through you guys."

Desmond turned his head as the roar of a gun firing sounded in his ears and a storm of bullets flew through the door toward Ciara. Her eyes met Desmond's with a look of surprise, fear, and then agony and she dropped to the floor.

"Ciara! NO!" Desmond ran to her as Agent Winston rushed the door while he shouted commands into his radio. "Shots fired, shots fired! We've got a woman down at the Ashler residence. Send an ambulance ASAP!"

Agent Green ran into the room through the adjoining door with his gun drawn, having heard the shots.

Desmond knelt beside Ciara, evaluating her injuries. There was blood everywhere. "I need something to put on this wound!" he shouted. "Get me some towels!" Seconds later someone handed large towels to him and Desmond took one, folded it, and laid it on the floor, gently rolling just enough to place the towel beneath her. He rolled her back onto the towel so her body would hold pressure on the larger wound on her back. He began applying pressure on the wound in her chest, but noticed there was frothy blood and a strange hissing sound coming from the wound.

"Plastic! I need a plastic bag!" he shouted and almost immediately a hotel laundry sack was dropped by his side. Using the pocket knife he always carried in his pants pocket, he quickly cut the sides and bottom of the sack, creating two flat pieces of plastic. Cutting open Ciara's shirt, front and back, he placed half the sack flat against the wound on her back when Ciara exhaled, in an attempt to mimic the vacuum in the chest cavity. Remembering his medical training he knew if that chest vacuum was breached, the lungs couldn't work correctly.

Rolling her onto her back, ensuring the towel was pressing the plastic firmly against the wound, he fitted the other half of the bag securely over the wound on her chest. The hissing sound stopped, and it seemed the next breath Ciara took was a little easier.

Several agents from the other floors had converged on their floor. There were voices calling down the hall, the sound of feet running. There was shouting, more calls for the ambulance to get there. All the while Desmond held the plastic, allowing air to escape from one side of the plastic each time Ciara exhaled and watching as each inhale sucked the plastic tight against the wound. He wondered how Ciara could survive this.

"Ciara, I don't know if you can hear me, baby, but hang in there. Help is coming; you have to hang in there. If you *can* hear me, listen to my voice, I won't stop talking to you, just listen to what I'm saying and don't leave me. Stay with me, Ciara, stay with me."

She was still breathing, and, occasionally her eyelids would flutter, as if she were trying to open her eyes, but they'd just roll back in her head and she'd go out again. Desmond kept talking to her, ignoring the chaos around him.

Soon a gurney was rolled swiftly into the room with several paramedics running along beside it. They tried to move Desmond, but he jerked his arm away and refused to leave her. He wasn't thinking clearly, he feared she would die when they took her and he wouldn't be there with her.

"Sir, listen to me. You've done a good job here, you'd done everything you could do, but we need to take over now. This is a serious wound. You *have* to let us help her. You're wasting precious seconds. Step back, sir, let us help her."

A soft sob escaped his lips as he stood and backed away. His hands were covered with Ciara's blood and he couldn't stop staring at them. Was this all he would have left of this amazing woman? Was this how he would remember her?

The paramedics taped Desmond's plastic bags securely in place, leaving one side untapped on the front. They placed IVs in her arms and lifted Ciara onto the gurney. They ran for the door and Desmond stayed with them.

"I'm with her," he said with finality.

The paramedics glanced quickly at one another and the same one spoke to him as before. "There's a lot that has to be done when we get her to the ambulance, sir, and very little room to do it in. You're going to need to ride in the second ambulance. We can't let you get in the way of saving her. Do you understand?"

"Yes."

The paramedic's words were distant and echoed through him as if he were hollow inside. All Desmond could see, all he could hear was Ciara. She was his world, and he would do whatever it took to keep her alive. If it meant riding in another ambulance, he would do that. They entered the service elevator and went down to the ground floor. As soon as the doors opened, the gurney was rushed to the ambulance. Desmond climbed into the back of the second ambulance and they raced to the hospital with lights flashing and siren blaring.

Desmond sat in the back, resting his elbows on his knees, staring at the blood on his hands. "Here, sir…Desmond, correct?" Desmond nodded. "Here, Desmond. Take these moist towels and wipe your hands."

It was a woman's voice and he looked up, thinking it was Ciara. For that split second his heart jumped thinking she was really okay, that this was just some kind of bad movie he'd been watching. But it was another paramedic and he took the towels and wiped his hands. He looked at the blood now on the towel and held the towel to his already blood-covered shirt.

Stay with me, Ciara. Don't leave me. Don't leave me.

Words floated softly into his head. "I'm here, my love. I'm here."

It was Ciara and Desmond held tighter to the blood-smeared towels, fighting the urge to scream out her name.

They arrived at the Emergency Department and Ciara was unloaded as Desmond watched. He hurried behind as the gurney was rolled at a full run into the building. He followed them to the doors where two attendants held him back.

One of them spoke to him. "You'll need to wait here, sir, I'm sorry."

Desmond watched his life roll down that long corridor and disappear into a room. He stood staring vacantly after it, aware only of the breaking of his heart.

"Desmond!" He turned to see Neo coming through the doors. "How is she?"

"I...I don't know," he said, staring into the eyes of his best friend. "There was so much blood, Neo. How can she live if she's lost that much blood? It was everywhere. I should have taken that bullet. It was meant for me, Neo. It was meant for *me*. *I'm* the one he's angry with. *It was meant for me.*"

Neo glanced around the waiting area and strode swiftly to the reception desk. He held up his badge. "I need a private room, right away."

The young receptionist stared up at him with wide, frightened eyes. "I'll come around and meet you at the double doors."

"Thank you."

Neo returned to Desmond and explained they were going to a private room. Desmond followed him through the same doors they'd taken Ciara. It was all he could do not to sprint down the hall and search each room until he found her. Neo knew immediately what he was thinking.

"She's already in surgery, Desmond. The only thing you can do is wait."

He instructed the attendant to make sure they received all updates as they came in. She nodded in agreement and left the room, closing the door behind her.

"Desmond, listen to me," began Neo. "You have to focus for me, right now. Can you answer some questions?"

Lights went on in Desmond's eyes. A look of fierce determination replaced the devastation of the few minutes before. "Yes. I can focus. Tell me what you need to know."

Chapter Three

When Andre Winston called to tell Neo of the shooting, the line went silent. After a few moments, the first question out of Neo's mouth was, "Where was Green?"

Agent Winston explained that Green had gone into the bathroom and left him to watch the monitors alone when the man approached the door with the wheeled serving tray. He explained as soon as he saw the man he called to Green, "Get out here, Green, we've got company." It was then he started into Desmond and Ciara's room. He said Desmond, who'd just heard the knock, met him in the doorway. He also said the last and only time he'd seen Green was when he ran into the room after the shot was fired. Winston said he ran into the hallway to help search when Green came into the room to stay with Desmond. Winston said he was met by several agents who'd heard the radio call and come as fast as they could. Winston then told Neo when he came back into the room several minutes later Green was gone and the EMTs showed up shortly after that.

Neo chose his words carefully as he sat with Desmond in the private room at the hospital.

"Desmond, how many people were in your room when the shots were fired?"

"Th..." Desmond's eyes searched for the answer. "Three. There were three of us. Agent Winston, Ciara and myself."

"Where did the shots come from?"

"The door. They came right through the main door into the suite. I was talking to Winston and Ciara...Ciara was...was standing in the living room. I'd gone to the adjoining door, which put me behind a wall. I was protected by the wall, so was Winston. Ciara was in the open with no shelter, nothing to hide behind. The shots were scattered across the room, but I'm pretty sure he only got Ciara once."

"Do you remember when Agent Green entered the room?"

"No, I didn't see him come in. Someone handed me towels and a plastic bag for the wound, but I didn't see who it was."

"You're doing great Desmond," said Neo. It was hard to question his friend like this, but it kept Desmond thinking, kept his mind going. "I just have a couple more questions. Can you remember if anyone opened your front door?"

"No, I wasn't looking," replied Desmond, still thinking. "Wait. Someone must have, because that's how the paramedics got in. They didn't break the door down. I was preoccupied, but I would have noticed *that*."

"Okay. How about Agent Green? Did you see him when you followed the gurney to the service elevator?"

"No."

Neo nodded. "Okay, that's all I've got for now. Hang in there, Desmond. Ciara is a strong person. She's going to pull through this."

"I'm going to kill him, Neo. I'm going to kill Bradford."

"Not if I get him first," said Neo solemnly. "But I don't think Bradford was the shooter. We have to tear the video apart frame by frame and see how much of the shooter we can see."

"Green?" Desmond's eyes grew fierce as the thought seared his brain. "Is that why you keep asking me about him?" There was fire there and Neo didn't want to fan those flames.

"I can't say yet, Desmond," said Neo. "We won't know for sure who it was until we can get the video analyzed."

Desmond sprang from his chair and began pacing. "What if she doesn't make it? What if she dies in there?" He pointed to the door accusingly.

"You can't think like that, Desmond. You have to keep yourself positive. She needs your strength right now because she's fighting with everything she's got to stay with you. You have to fight to stay with her, too. She needs you to be strong for her."

Neo watched the fight drain from his friend. Desmond sank down into a stiff hospital easy chair in the corner of the small room. He nodded in agreement and laid his head back, staring at the ceiling. Somehow he would be there for Ciara. Somehow, he would make himself *know* she would make it. As soon as the thought formed in his head, he began to see the blood on her clothes, on the carpet, on the towels. There was blood everywhere; on his hands, his shirt, his jeans. It was all over him, all over her, all over the room.

He squeezed his eyes shut and made himself focus on the last lesson he'd taken at shooting range. He'd stared at the target until it was fixed in his head and he'd made a perfect shot. He forced his mind back to the moment before she walked away from him in the hotel, he remembered the joy on her face, holding her in his arms and her excitement of going back to work again. He held the love he saw in her eyes above everything else he'd seen that day. *That* was his target. It was Ciara, strong, vibrant, and very much alive. She would return to him, stronger than before, and he would help *her* recover this time.

***

Neo watched his friend struggle through the agony Neo knew he was feeling. He couldn't help but relate to Desmond. It made him think of his dream. And his dream, for some reason, made him think of Agent Green. Where did that come from? It felt random to Neo, disjointed, out of sync.

Green was a piece that had to fit in somewhere. He was missing, gone, disappeared. It was like he'd evaporated into thin air. There were agents who came up from other floors, some by the stairs, some by the elevators. No one saw him leave, but he was gone by the time the paramedics arrived.

If Green was the shooter, and was working for Bradford, what did this mean for Emmett? Green knew just as much about Emmett's operation as the rest of the team. He could easily get the information to Bradford and expose Emmett. If, in fact, Green *was* working for Bradford that would mean Emmett was in grave danger. Knowing that, there was just something in Neo that rejected the idea of Green working both sides. Cayman held the man in the highest regard, and Cayman was pretty picky about his 'high regard.'

As soon as the attack on Desmond and Ciara came through the radio, more agents were assigned to Neo's building. Patrick and Sam were placed inside the penthouse and several other agents were stationed in the hallway outside the home and in front of the door. The elevator and stairs to the top floor were shut down. Unless he was Spiderman, there was no way anyone was getting into the penthouse. But that didn't stop Neo from worrying.

Desmond sat forward and rubbed both hands over his face. Suddenly, a thought struck Neo as he watched his friend.

"Desmond, think hard for a minute. Who handed you those towels?"

"I didn't even look up, Neo, I just took the towels and used them."

"And, what about the plastic laundry bag? Who handed you that?"

"I just yelled that I needed the bag and it was almost immediately by my side."

"Think, Desmond. Did you see shoes, a pant leg, a hand? Anything?"

"No, nothing. Why?"

Neo stopped and thought for a minute. "Oh, it's probably nothing. I've got to go make a call, are you okay here for a minute?"

"Yeah, yeah, I'm fine."

Neo stepped quickly into the hall and stood outside the door of the room they were in. He dialed Cayman.

"How's he doing?" said Cayman when he picked up his phone.

"As well as can be expected, I'd guess. But, Cayman, I have a theory. I don't want to leave Desmond so I need agents in their apartment. I think Green hid in there until he could escape without being seen. He may have been seen leaving on the monitors in the adjoining room. I think he was there the whole time."

"What makes you say that?"

"Because Desmond says that Winston ran into the hallway and left Green with them. He said someone handed him towels to help with Ciara, but Desmond never looked up or made eye contact. I'm betting it was Green. I'm also betting Green was the shooter and I want that hotel room searched inch by inch."

"Green is a good man, Neo. I've worked with him for years. I'd have a hard time believing he would be capable of something like this."

"Cayman, anyone can be seduced by greed. Anyone." Neo's voice was somber. He'd learned that concept first hand.

"I'll get some men over there. In fact, I'll go over with them. The only way I'll believe this is to see the evidence myself."

"Thanks. I've got to get back in there and stay with Desmond. I don't think he should be by himself for very long." Neo started to end the call and stopped. "Oh, and Cayman?"

"Yeah."

"If Green is at large, if he even *might possibly* be the shooter, that means he's working for Bradford, and it means we've got to figure out how many people are at risk by that relationship, especially Emmett."

"We'll take care of it, Neo. You take care of Desmond."

The call ended and Neo returned to their private waiting room.

***

Cayman and Winston stepped into the suite with guns drawn, silently making their way to the living room. The first thing Cayman saw was blood, a lot of blood, and it made his stomach turn to think it belonged to Ciara.

Cayman nodded silently for Winston to continue checking the room and he continued down the short hallway and into the first bedroom. He searched carefully, opening the closet doors slowly, checking under the bed. The room was clean. He proceeded then to the second bedroom and met Winston in the hall. He motioned for Winston to come with him into the second bedroom.

Once inside the room, the men heard movement in the closet. Cayman pointed to the door and, standing to the side, Winston opened the door. Cayman, who had his gun pointed in the direction of the sound, immediately relaxed and lowered his gun.

"Winston, help me out." Cayman holstered his gun and knelt down. Jay Green was curled up in a fetal position, sweating profusely and talking to himself.

"Jay, it's me, Cayman, let me help you out of the closet." He reached out to take Jay's arm and the man let go an agonizing, guttural sound.

"Make them stop, it's too much noise. Make them stop."

"Let me help you, Jay. Here, take my hand. Andre will take the other hand. Come on Jay, we can help you stop the noise. Let us help you."

Once they had Agent Green out of the closet, Cayman nodded to Winston. "Call an ambulance."

Jay Green's face was pale, beyond pale. He looked like someone had painted his face white. His eyes were red and bloodshot, and he was drooling uncontrollably.

Green suddenly sat up and grabbed Cayman by both shoulders. "Stop the noise! Stop it! It's too loud. I can't think. Can't think. Too loud."

Cayman saw several needle marks in his left arm. "Who did this to you, Jay? Who made these marks in your arm?"

Agent Green's red eyes never left Cayman's face. "Too loud, stop the noise. You're…you're melting. Don't melt, don't leave me. *Don't melt!*"

Winston came back into the room and Cayman looked up at him. "Help me get him off the floor. We can lay him on the bed. He's got needle marks in his arms and he's hallucinating. He's been drugged."

As they laid him out on the bed, Agent Green immediately assumed the fetal position once again, almost like he was trying to protect himself. After only a few minutes, Cayman heard the paramedics call from the doorway.

"In here!" yelled Cayman. "Hurry!"

As the paramedics prepped Agent Green for transport, Cayman pointed out the needle marks in his arm. One of them, who'd been checking him for wounds said, "He's got something in his ear." Then, turning Jay's head, he said, "There's one in both ears." Speaking to the other paramedic he said, "I'm going to bag these. Hand me a bag and some tweezers."

As soon as the earpieces came out of his ears, Agent Green visibly relaxed. The muscles in Cayman's jaw moved back and forth, his mouth was clenched tightly. He finally spoke. "He's not only been drugged, someone was messing with his mind. What kind of messed up freak does something like this to another human being?" Cayman reached for the bag with the evidence in it. "I'll take those."

The paramedic handed the bag to Cayman.

Jay was rolled out of the room and to the service elevator. Cayman rode down with them and Winston stayed at the suite to help with the investigation.

This was about as near to losing it as Cayman had ever come. He watched his friend wheeled out to the waiting ambulance. *Bradford is going to pay for what he's done. He's going to pay.*

Cayman pulled his phone from his pocket and quickly dialed Jennifer.

"This is Jennifer."

"Hey, Jen, it's me. I want an all-points out for Bradford. We're going public with him…as public as we can get him. I want him on the most wanted list, and I want every law enforcement employee, from FBI agents to meter maids, to know he's out there. Put a $500,000 reward on his head for information leading to his arrest. If the Bureau won't back it, I'm sure Neo will. Just get it done."

"Yes, sir."

Chapter Four

Ciara was out of surgery and recovery and in her own room when they allowed Desmond to finally see her. The nurse cautioned him on her ability to respond to him.

"She is heavily sedated and she may not hear you speaking to her, but talk to her anyway. Sometimes it's comforting to hear the voice of a loved one. Let her know you're here. If you would like to read her a book, just so she can hear your voice, let me know. I'd be happy to bring you something to read to her."

Desmond nodded as the nurse turned to go. "Nurse?"

"Yes?" She said, stopped and turning to face Desmond.

"Will she live? Is she going to be okay?"

"The doctor will be here shortly. He'll answer all your questions." The nurse left, closing the door behind her.

Desmond looked down at Ciara, so beautiful even when she slept. He picked up her hand and held it gently in his.

"Been kind of a long day, eh?" he said, smiling weakly. "You shouldn't have taken that bullet, Ciara. I'll spend the rest of my life apologizing to you for that. I'm so sorry."

Desmond kissed her hand and held it against his cheek. "What do you say we head to Hawaii when you're better? I could sure do with that. You know, I'm going to take care of *you* this time. I'm sure you won't be as wonderful a patient as I was, but I'll try to be kind." Desmond's face softened and his voice sank to a whisper. "Come back to me, Ciara. I'm going to stay right here until you do. Come back to me."

The doctor opened the door and entered the room. His gray hair was combed back and he wore dark-rimmed glasses. Shorter than Desmond, he looked to be in his late forties or early fifties. "I'm Dr. Schilling, Mr…"

Desmond stood and shook the doctor's hand. "Ashler, Desmond Ashler. Ciara is my fiancée."

"She's a very lucky girl, Mr. Ashler. This could have been much worse than it was. The bullet nicked her lung but missed major arteries. Came pretty close, but even a tiny miss is still a miss when it comes to arteries. We'll remove the chest tube probably by tomorrow. Her oxygen saturation was normal by the end of her stay in recovery and she was breathing on her own so we took her off oxygen before bringing her to her room. Her progress is really quite remarkable."

Desmond relaxed visibly. "How soon will she wake up, Doctor?"

Dr. Schilling gazed down on his patient. "Hard to say, anywhere from an hour to six hours. But from what I've seen of her, it shouldn't be too long. Do you have any other questions for me?"

"No, thank you for filling me in."

"You're very welcome. Just press that little button at the top of her bed to call for a nurse if you need anything. There's another button on her remote."

"Thanks."

Desmond bent over and kissed Ciara's forehead. She was going to make it. She would be just fine. The relief he felt was like nothing he'd ever experienced. He sat down in the chair beside her bed and started talking to her again.

"I know this place in Hawaii, it's got the most beautiful view of the ocean...."

***

"Lysergic acid diethylamide."

Dr. Wyland stood at the end of Jay Green's bed with a clipboard under one arm as he spoke to Cayman. His dark hair was made almost black in the dimmed light, the same with his eyes. He spoke with a slight accent.

"LSD? This was caused by LSD?"

"Yes, and the small speakers in his ears simply added to the experience. He was being fed instructions and once the deed was done, I'm guessing the noise was supposed to drive him over the edge to insanity, causing him to turn the gun on himself. He's one strong man to be able to withstand that. I've given him a sedative to help him sleep for a while. He should be out for a few hours yet."

"Thank you, Doctor," said Cayman, then remembering a question he had, he said, "Doctor

Wyland, can you tell me...will he remember his experiences while under the influence of the drug?"

"Some do and some don't. There is no exact answer for that. You'll just have to wait and see."

"Okay, thanks."

"Just holler if you need anything."

"Will do."

Cayman decided he would have the nurse's station give him a call when Jay woke up. There was a certain amount of relief that came with knowing the man he'd come to trust with his life had most likely been unaware of his actions. However, explaining that to Desmond was going to be rough.

***

Bradford spent the day on his computer and cell phone, testing his contacts and attempting to determine who was still there, who was still loyal and who would turn him in if the money was good enough.

As he laid his phone on the table, he stared at the computer screen. Fully aware his network was gone, he was beginning to feel the squeeze of having his face plastered all over the news and in every law enforcement office in the country. He was now on the FBI most wanted list and this wasn't good. He definitely needed someone to help him...he needed Emmett Matisse.

He opened his email and began typing. He had to word it just right. He definitely didn't want to sound desperate.

***

Emmett was beginning to think Bradford hadn't bought his story. He'd emailed every rogue address he could remember for Bradford, checked places he would go when he needed time away, all the places only Bradford and Tipton knew about. Unbeknownst to Bradford, Emmett was aware of these places due to his relationship with Tipton.

But now, if Bradford wasn't going to buy into the story of the prison break and his loyalty to Tipton and thus Bradford, then the Bureau would've gone through all of this for nothing. Having heard nothing back from him wasn't a good sign.

Emmett closed the lid on his laptop and laid it on the bed. As he turned to stand, he heard something he'd not heard in a very long time. It was the chime of an incoming email. Whipping his feet back up on the bed, he turned and leaned back against the headboard once more. He placed his computer on his lap and opened the lid. Sure enough, he'd received an email.

The name on the screen was unfamiliar and obviously coded, but he clicked on it and the email burst onto the screen. The note was from Bradford. He was certain of it, disappointed, but certain.

"The cowboys are closing in. You won't be a free to roam for long. No more room in this corral. Stay away."

Right. Like that is going to happen.

Emmett thought for a few minutes about what he wanted to say and how to say it and began typing.

"Cowboys are as close to you as they are to me. I know, because I was a cowboy once. You were

always just a farmer, never knew the details of the herd. You need me."

Once he hit send, Emmett stared at the screen for several minutes before closing the laptop once again. He stood and strode to the window, standing beside it and peeking out through the curtains. He'd not seen anyone watching the room that he could tell, but he liked to check every once in a while just to be sure. He wanted to make sure Bradford hadn't somehow figured out where he was staying. It was surreal the way he could find people.

Emmett took his daily 'outing,' for his update from the Bureau. This time he'd be actually speaking with someone, though he'd not been told who would meet him. He was to go to a specific bench inside Fort Dupont State Park and wait on the bench to be contacted.

Emmett picked up a newspaper at the front desk and headed to his car. Once at the park, he located the park bench and sat down, glancing casually around the park. The requested bench was actually two in one, sitting back to back with a good view of the park from either side. Emmett watched people in the park for a while and then picked up the newspaper and began browsing through it.

A few minutes passed before he felt someone sit down on the bench behind him. Ignoring the newcomer, he continued reading. He heard a newspaper unfolding and pages turning.

"This park needs work," said a male voice behind him.

"I agree, we should complain."

With the meet established, the real conversation began.

"Have you made contact?"

"Yes, but I'm waiting for him to respond. His first response was negative, wanted to stay away from me. I'm hoping to have heard something when I get back."

"Do you suspect he's aware of the mission?"

"No, he's just being cautious."

The contact stood and folded his newspaper under his arm and left. Emmett continued to read for another half hour. Eventually, he glanced down at his watch, folded his paper, and sat for another few minutes watching the people again before getting up and leaving. He grabbed some lunch from a fast food drive-thru and headed back to his room, taking a different route than the one he'd used when he left.

The parking lot was nearly empty and Emmett parked, exited the car and entered the motel room. He went right to the laptop and found there was an email waiting for him. It was from Bradford.

You talk big, Cowboy, but you ended up in the kettle. How can I know you won't get me in the same stew? I watched the herd very carefully, I was the first to bolt, remember? How do I know I can trust you?

Emmett closed the lid on the laptop and paced the room for a few minutes. How should he respond to that? What did he want to say? He wasn't sure, and needed a few minutes to read through the messages and see if there was anything in them he'd missed. They all appeared very straightforward at first read.

He sat down on the bed and reread the emails. He saw no secondary messages in them. He read them over several times, ran a code breaker program through them and concluded the same thing. They were clean.

His response had to be direct. He must make Bradford believe he needed Emmett for his own protection. He put his fingers to the keyboard and began typing.

"I've been doing this cowboy thing for a lot of years. I've covered a lot of territory, rounded up a lot of herds. Also kept watch on individual steers. I know what I'm doing. As a farmer, you haven't been in the herd for many years. You'd be wise to accept my offer. I'm not keeping it out there long. I'm up for the highest bidder at this point."

He closed out of email and shut the laptop. Once he got a confirmed meet, he could let the Bureau know and this whole fiasco would be done. He was anxious to be back to his own clean apartment and his comfy bed.

***

Cayman closed the door softly and let his eyes adjust to the dim light. Ciara was asleep and Desmond's head lay on the bed, a soft snore escaping with each breath. He hated to disturb Desmond, but he desperately need to talk to him. He walked to the side of the bed and softly laid his hand on his friend's shoulder.

Desmond jumped and Cayman shushed him. He nodded for Desmond to follow him into the hallway.

"Have you caught Bradford?" Desmond was still wiping the sleep from his eyes, trying to wake up. He felt like he hadn't had a full night's sleep for days. Had it really only been hours since her surgery?

"No, not yet. How is Ciara doing?"

"She's starting to stir every once in a while. They think she'll be coming around pretty soon." Desmond's eyes were bloodshot and drooped with fatigue.

"You really should go home and get some sleep. You need to rest. If you get sick you won't be allowed in here, you know." Cayman had to say it, even though he knew if their situations were reversed he'd be doing the exact same thing.

"I know, I know. I just can't bring myself to leave her. What's up? Have you heard anything?"

"Let's have a seat, I do need to talk to you." Cayman motioned to a sofa outside the patient rooms.

"We found out the shooter wasn't exactly Bradford."

"Wasn't exactly? What does that mean?"

Cayman searched Desmond's face. "What I mean is, he prepped the shooter, shot him full of LSD and then stuck a small unit in his ear that made him do whatever was repeated. We think the shooter's brain malfunctioned and instead of following protocol he shot blindly through the door and hit Ciara."

"Who's 'he'? Desmond was staring at his hands, the muscles in his jaw working back and forth.

"Agent Jay Green."

Desmond sat back on the sofa and rubbed his hands over his face. "Jay Green? One of our bodyguards?"

"Yes. We haven't been able to ascertain how Bradford got a hold of him, but he did somehow and messed him up pretty good. He's in the hospital now, we're hoping to get some questions answered." Cayman stared at Desmond. "It wasn't his fault,

Desmond. You know he'd never have done anything like this on his own accord."

"Yeah, yeah. I know. I appreciate you telling me. I'll be fine, just need to digest this for a while. I gotta get back to Ciara."

Desmond stood and strode back into Ciara's room. Cayman knew he'd best keep a sharp eye on him for a while. Hopefully he really did understand.

Chapter Five

Bradford arranged for a meeting at his cabin in a wooded area outside of D.C. He'd texted the location to Emmett when they set up the meet the previous day. Bradford was still smiling at the secluded neighborhood. It would be difficult, if not impossible to get back up into the area without being seen.

"If he's playing both sides, this location should make him squirm a little." Bradford grinned as he pulled into the dirt drive of the cabin and shut off the engine. He sat back in his seat as his coal dark eyes stared at the cabin.

There was so much history that went with this cabin. People died here, always at his hand, and he'd been happy to see them go. The three bodies, found in a running car in a garage belonging to one of them, had also been his doing. He thought it a stroke of genius to make it look like a suicide. Truly.

It was a hard decision to kill Gus Atkinson, however. He was the only non-agent among all the rogue team. He'd been so very useful, so eager to help. He was hired on as a janitorial assistant to the Housekeeping Supervisor. He was given keys to every office, as he was assigned, not just as an assistant, but as a 'roving' housekeeper, filling in when anyone called in sick or when the rogue team had a *need* to have access to an office. He was a nice guy, but in spite of that, he was a little *too* eager to please. Had a connection to him been made Bradford feared he would've spilled his guts to anyone who would listen. He had to go.

Then there was Ethan Williams. Good agent, truly felt like the NSA was moving in the wrong direction, filled with conspiracy theories, he was the easiest of all to recruit. The theories were already in place in his mind. Bradford had only to build on what was there and Williams was hooked. The only problem with Williams was he was so very anxious to prove himself right he'd have blown the whole operation if given the chance, just to prove his point. He would've told them everything, thinking he was showing how he'd single-handedly fixed the NSA. Idiot.

And last of all, Harrison Hatchler. So-so agent, loyal like a sheep dog, very little ability to think on his feet. Along with that small ability came a certain amount of 'buffoon.' He felt little, so he talked big. That pretty much summed it up. If he could say something or know something that made him feel superior, he'd spill it all just to look like the big man. He definitely couldn't live to tell his tale.

Bradford invited them all to this very cabin to do the deed. He was sure by this time the FBI had discovered the poison in their systems. He'd strangled them as well, just before they'd died, thinking the ligature marks would be as far as the authorities would look. It wasn't, and he should have known better. He was pretty certain the poison had been traced to him by now. Ah, well…as they say, 'the best laid plans.' At the very least he may have bought himself a little extra time.

He regretted putting that note in Harrison's pocket. Thinking it a good idea at the time, now he realized it ruined the whole idea of suicide. He just wanted Neo to know he meant business, and that one way or another he was going to get what he came back for. Though he'd hoped to make it look like a suicide, once the note was read, it wouldn't. But maybe, just maybe it would be confusing enough to keep them guessing for a day or two. No, probably not. It'd been a stupid thing to do.

Bradford's uneasy mind came to rest on Emmett Matisse, aka Michael McPheeters. Would he let him live? He'd hacked into the prison system and read Matisse's file. A troublemaker from the beginning, he was placed in prison as a flight risk. It was clear to Bradford, Matisse felt superior to all the murderers and thugs in there, having been an FBI agent. He'd picked fights, argued, even bullied the guards, held a complete disregard for rules and regs of 'the big house,' and spent an inordinate amount of time in lockdown. He'd basically thumbed his nose at the prison world. Bradford kind of liked this guy.

There was concern on Bradford's part about Matisse's breaking out of prison. It appeared he'd escaped using the old 'hide in the laundry bin' trick. Bradford had a hard time believing he'd escaped on his own. He had to have gotten help from someone, and because of that, the whole thing smelled of FBI. If the FBI was involved, Bradford was already caught. He had to be careful with this one. If he was who he said he was, Matisse would be very useful. If not, he could be deadly. Working with him was a gamble, and Bradford was a gambler. It's how he'd gotten where he was in life, and it paid very well.

Exiting the car, he walked to the cabin and unlocked the door. Imagine his surprise to see Emmett Matisse sitting at the kitchen table helping himself to a can of peaches.

"Sorry, you were taking too long and I was hungry. There are a few left, you want some?" Emmett casually shoved the can toward Bradford.

"How did you get in here?"

"Like any good FBI agent worth his salt, I picked the lock on the back door. It was pretty easy. Hope you don't mind. Oh, and your bread is stale. How old is that loaf anyway? You seriously need some groceries."

Bradford studied him, keeping his concerns to himself. "There's fresh food in the freezer on the back stoop. Did you check there?"

"No, should have. But I found these peaches and that was enough for the moment. So, tell me what you need. Are you heading out of the country? You got money?"

"I'll tell you what you need to know if I decide this little arrangement is going to work. For now, I ask the questions and you answer them. Clear?"

"Gotcha. Ask away."

Bradford pulled out a kitchen chair and sat down, never taking his eyes from Matisse. He waited a few moments to start. It was obvious Matisse had all the time in the world.

"How do I know I can trust you?"

"Depends on what you're trusting me with, I guess. If you think I'm going to clean myself up and go crawling back to the FBI, I wouldn't trust that. Besides, I hardly think that would be prudent, do you?"

"I'm trusting you with my life, should we decide to partner up."

"Then, yes, you can trust me. And how do you know that? I guess if my past record doesn't speak for itself, then you can't. Don't know what to tell you. But as I see it, because of the nature of our business, only one of us is going to leave here alive unless we come out of the cabin as partners. Is that how you see it?"

"I suppose. Hadn't really thought about it."

Emmett laughed a large rolling belly laugh at the comment. "Oh sure," he chuckled. "You hadn't thought of that. Right. You've already figured four different ways to kill me." Emmett abruptly stopped laughing and threw his spoon on the table as he leaned forward and stared hard into Bradford's dark eyes. "Well listen up, *Mr. Bradford*. I've got two different ways to kill you for every one of yours. Got that? If only one of us is leaving alive, it's gonna be me."

Bradford frowned, until it began to look as if he was trying very hard not to laugh. Suddenly a laugh burst out of him and he leaned on the table.

"Something funny?" Emmett was a little irritated.

"You know," Bradford said, his laughter subsiding, "I was always a little jealous of Tipton that he found you first. I like you, Matisse. I've always liked you. Let's just say we're partners." He stuck out his hand and Emmett smiled and shook it.

"So, why don't you fill me in as to why you're still in the States. Everyone else split to parts unknown, didn't they?" Emmett folded his arms and leaned back in his seat.

"Well, you could say that, but to my knowledge, I'm the only one that's evaded arrest at this point. I could leave the States now and live very well, but I want that encryption code Neo Weston carries around in his head. That code is worth *billions* and if we could get our hands on it, we could offer it to the highest bidder and live pretty fat the rest of our lives."

"You have a plan for that? From what I understand his house is a fortress, he's never out on his own, which makes it harder…"

Bradford interrupted him. "It may have been nearly impossible with only one of us, but now that there are two, we might be able to take out the agent or agents he's with and grab him."

"You know we're talking about the former Justin Markham, right? The sniper and cryptology savant?"

"Yes, well, we will have to come up with a plan. Where are you staying?"

"I'm at a creepy little motel in D.C. Certainly not what I'm used to, but I've been keeping a low profile. And of course, I have a good disguise, part of which you can see I'm not using right now. I left my beard in my room. I didn't want you to shoot me before we could talk."

"Good plan." Bradford smiled. "I think this is going to work out very nicely. Go clean out your place." He handed Emmett a bulky envelope. Emmett looked inside and his eyes widened. "Get yourself a nicer place. I want us to continue to live separately, but stay in close contact. I've got your email address, you've got mine, and we'll meet several times a week to formulate a plan for getting Weston. Once I have him, and have the encryption code, we'll offer it to the highest bidder, split the proceeds, and we'll go our separate ways."

"Sounds good to me. You talkin' fifty/fifty?"

Bradford considered his new partner across the table. "I'm more inclined to a seventy/thirty split."

"Well, I'm not so inclined. I'm taking as big a risk as you are with this. Fifty/fifty or nothing."

Bradford smiled his sickening sweet smile. He knew Emmett wouldn't live long enough to enjoy any kind of split. He intended to kill his new partner before it ever came to that. "Fifty/fifty it is."

The two men shook hands again and Emmett left the way he'd come in, heading into the trees behind the cabin. He'd parked just on the other side of the trees, off the main road.

Bradford cleared off the table, threw out the stale bread and left shortly after Emmett.

He walked out to his car and climbed in, sitting once again and thinking, this time about the meeting. He was certain Emmett was someone who was going to work out very well. He needed to get this job done quickly. Their next meeting would cement a plan he'd had in his head for quite some time. Now that there were two of them, Bradford felt the plan would come off without a hitch. Things were coming together quite nicely.

He hated the thought of killing Emmett when the need for him was over, but sometimes things just had to be a certain way. There was no way he was going to split anything with anyone. This was *his* op from the beginning and he'd worked very hard to get it this far. It's just a good thing he had so many contingency plans in place. He'd needed every one of them.

***

"Did you get that?" Emmett got into his car, checked the area and started it up, heading back out to the main road.

"Yes, the bugs worked perfectly in the cabin, and your ear implant comes through clean." Agent Van Bingham was answering Emmett's inquiry. "We want a better sense of how this is all going to go down, once we have that, we're good to go."

"Well, just don't wait too long. Neo's life depends on us getting the specifics quickly."

Emmett swung the car out onto the main road. The call from the Bureau ended and left him alone with his thoughts.

Why don't they just swoop in and grab him? What's the delay? Now we're talking about a timeline that could be very dangerous for Neo. What are they waiting for?

Emmett pulled out his sat phone and dialed Cayman. He spoke using a Bluetooth headset so he wouldn't need to hold on to a phone. It was more covert that way, less telling to anyone who may be watching him.

"Richards."

"Hey, Cayman, it's Emmett."

"I hear your meet went well."

"Wow, news travels fast over there, doesn't it? Yeah, it went well, but I'm concerned about Neo. So far what I know is he plans to kill any agents who are with Neo once his plan is in place, then he'll get the code from him, and kill Neo. How he's planning on doing that, I don't know yet. Maybe he'll use me as a decoy. I just think we need to get him before this comes down."

"I know," replied Cayman. "But you have to look at it from a court's point of view. We need solid evidence of what he's done. A confession would be nice. That way, all the devastation he's caused won't look like random violence, but will be tied together in a nice, neat package, one that shows premeditation with intent. We want the strongest conviction we can get, Emmett, and if we're going to get it, we have to have hard evidence.

"I understand, but it makes me nervous. I'll keep you posted."

The call ended and once again Emmett was alone with his thoughts. The money in that envelope had to be close to ten grand. He couldn't help but wonder if that was skimmed from Neo's family. He knew Neo would gladly pay it, if it meant getting this man out of his life once and for all. Emmett would just have take good care of it, so it could one day be returned to its rightful owner.

Chapter Six

Ciara's eyes slowly opened. The first thing she saw was Desmond's head resting on her bed. Her hand was in his, and she moved her pointer finger, tapping the back of his hand with it.

Desmond's eyes opened and he watched the finger tapping his hand. Slowly, the implication dawned on him and he sat straight up, a wide smile on his face.

"There you are," he began. "How are you feeling?"

"I'm good. I'm so glad you're here."

"I never left, as you can tell by my smell."

"Oh, I thought that was just the hospital smell." Ciara smiled weakly, her eyes closing. "Sleepy…"

Desmond bent over and kissed her forehead. "Sleep well, my love. I'll be right here."

A whisper escaped her lips as she nodded off. "No, go home and shower."

Desmond picked up the bed remote and pressed the call button.

"Yes?"

"Ciara woke up. She's gone back to sleep, but she woke up."

"Thank you."

Desmond sat back down and stared at Ciara. It was the greatest feeling to hear her speak. She'd recognized him, even joked with him. She was going to be okay. He picked up the bedside phone and called Neo.

"Weston."

"Hey, tell Cayman Ciara is awake. Well, *was* awake. She's gone back to sleep now."

"That's good news, Desmond. I know Cayman said he'd talked to you. How are you feeling about the shooting?"

"Ciara is awake, she spoke to me, teased me a little, and then fell back to sleep. I don't care about anything else. I'm so thankful she's alive and she recognized me. Nothing else matters."

"I know how you feel. I'll let Cayman know. We'll come by later this afternoon and see her."

"Thanks. She'll like that."

Desmond hung up the phone and sat down. Ciara stirred in her bed, her legs moved and she tried to turn over and winced with pain.

"Hey, slow down there, girl. You don't need to go moving around like that."

"Well, with all the girl chatter over there I can't get any sleep." Her eyes were sleepy, only half open, but she was smiling. "Was any one else hurt?"

"Not as bad as you, but yes, an agent was wounded. He's going to be fine."

The nurse came into the room and began checking monitors and adjusting the IV. Everything looked good and she nodded to Desmond. "The doctor will make his rounds this afternoon and check in on her."

"Thank you."

The nurse strolled out of the room and Desmond sat back down.

"I thought I told you to go home and shower."

Ciara was trying to stay awake and clearly needed to sleep. She was in and out of sleep, trying to force herself awake.

"Maybe I'll go shower if you'll go back to sleep. Stop trying to stay awake. You need to rest."

"Looks who's talking."

Desmond grinned and shook his head. There was no arguing with this woman. She always had to have the last word…even with a bullet hole in her chest. The thought made the grin dissipate. He took her hand in his and kissed it softly.

"Don't ask me to leave you, Ciara. I can't do it. I'm here and I'll be here until I bring you home."

***

Two days had passed since the shooting and Jay Green lay in his hospital bed staring at the ceiling. Those past two days were a blur of chaotic sounds and noises and each time Jay tried to figure out what had happened to him, the blur threatened to take him away again.

There were FBI agents outside his door. Was it for his protection or was he under arrest? He forced himself to stop thinking about it, but his mind would not obey. He wrestled with what he could remember, rolling it over in his mind until his mind threatened to turn on him. What happened to him? He remembered telling Andre he had to use the bathroom and…no…it began before that. He'd gone downstairs to get a sandwich at the shop next door to the hotel. The next thing he knew, he was going into the bathroom in the hotel room. From that point on his memory was noise and chaos. And towels.

Towels? What did that mean? White motel room towels. He must have used towels in the bathroom, which made sense, but why would he remember that? His brain fought to recall the events, but it was as if there was nothing in there. Everything was a blank. What had happened to him?

A nurse came through the door. "How are you feeling Mr. Green?"

"I…I don't know. I…I can't remember anything."

"That's pretty normal for what you've been through."

"What have I been through? What happened to me?"

"The doctor will be in this afternoon and will review your chart with you. Until then, just try to sleep. You need to rest."

Jay lay still once again, trying desperately to remember. Colors swirled in his head, people stretched and distorted mixing in with those colors. Guns firing, people running, towels…white fluffy towels. There was a complete picture there somewhere, but he lay in bed unable to see it. He became more frustrated, the longer he lay there not even realizing he'd shrunk into a fetal position and was mumbling to himself.

Eventually someone walked into his room, the visitor's body melting into the colors that swam freely in his head. Slowly his mind began to clear at the sound of a male voice. He swam through the colors and the disfigured people, trying to get back to the hospital room.

"Jay, look at my finger. I want you to focus on my finger. Can you see it?"

Jay could barely hear the words, but the voice sounded 'normal' to him and so he fought to hear and see. Slowly, the colors faded and a single pointer finger came into his view. Blurry at first, it slowly began to take shape. His muscles began to relax and it felt like he could breathe better.

"Yes, yes," he whispered. "I can see it."

"Hi Jay, do you know who I am?"

"Yes. I…I think so. You're…you're Dr. Kenning."

"That's right, Jay, very good. You've most likely been having some trouble remembering what happened to you. Do you remember anything at all?"

"Not really. When I try, my thoughts just turn into soup and I can't seem to focus on any one thing."

"Let me explain what happened as I understand it," Leon paused, taking a deep breath before beginning again. "At some point prior to the events in the hotel room, you were injected with LSD and implanted with small devices in your ears that fed you 'instructions,' if you will. That's why you're having such a difficult time sorting through those events. I would like to help you remember, if you're okay with that."

"You can help me remember? How?"

"I'd like to hypnotize you and see if we can loosen some of the memory fragments. Are you willing to try that?"

"Yes. Yes, I'd appreciate any help."

Leon moved one of the big chairs closer to the bed and instructed Jay regarding the procedure. He fluffed Jay's pillow and made sure he was comfortable, then sat down beside the bed.

"I want you to close your eyes and listen to the sound of my voice. That's right. Close your eyes. Now think about your most pleasant memory. Go back there, remember the feeling of the memory. Think about what you liked the most about the experience. Enjoy the feeling."

Jay's breathing became smooth and even. He face calmed and the muscles in his body completely relaxed.

"Keep relaxing Jay, you're calm and you're safe. Nothing can harm you." Leon spoke in an even, quiet voice until Jay was in a deep hypnotic trance.

"Jay, two days ago, you were involved in a shooting, but now you're safe. Nothing you remember will upset you. You will listen to the sound of my voice and answer my questions freely, but you will remain relaxed.

"Now, I want you to go back to the day of the shooting. Go back through the images you've been seeing, back before they began. Relax and let your mind take you back to that day."

The patient's eyebrows knitted and his hands formed fists.

"Relax your fingers, Jay, relax your arms. Tell me what you see, Jay."

"I...I'm in the hallway, I see the door into Desmond's room. Noise, so much noise."

"I want you to breathe deeply, now, Jay, and I want you to tell me what you hear. What kind of noise is it?"

"A voice. A loud voice."

"What is the voice telling you, Jay?"

"Shoot. It keeps saying shoot."

"Who are you supposed to shoot."

"It's wrong. I can't shoot. It's telling me to shoot Desmond. I can't shoot Desmond." Jay gasped and grabbed the blankets on his bed.

"You're safe Jay, I'm here with you. Breathe deeply and relax. Once you're completely relaxed and feel safe, I want you to tell me what you see."

"Bradford. Tristan Bradford is standing in front of Desmond's room door. He's yelling at me, screaming. He's telling me to kill Desmond. I don't want to kill Desmond. I want to kill Bradford. I raise my gun and point it at Bradford. He's right there. He's standing right in front of me. I fired my weapon and…I fired my weapon…over and over again. He wouldn't die. I had to keep firing until he finally…disappeared. He was gone. There was no body."

Jay began shaking and the shaking grew as he began screaming, "Who did I kill? WHO DID I KILL? I can't find a body, the voice tells me to go back into the bathroom in our surveillance room. I can't find a body. I go back into the bathroom. Who did I kill?"

Jay's body began shaking so violently his words were no longer clear. Leon jumped from his chair and placed his hands on both of Jay's arms. "Jay, I'm going to count to three and when I get to three you're going to wake up. You'll remember everything, but you'll be calm and free of fear. One. Two. Three."

Jay gasped and his eyes stared at the ceiling, his body went limp. Eventually his eyes met Leon's gaze and he shuddered.

"I was shooting Bradford. That's why I shot at the door. Bradford was standing there. He wanted me to shoot Desmond, but I knew that was wrong. I wouldn't do it. Bradford needed to be stopped and so I shot *him*."

Leon listened silently. He understood now why the bullets were shot through a closed door. It wasn't random. He knew who Jay was really shooting at.

Jay continued. "But I didn't shoot Bradford, did I? I shot…I shot Ciara." His eyes widened as the realization of what he'd done hit him. "Towels…I was handing towels to Desmond. He asked for a plastic bag and for more towels. I got them for him. I was working as hard as I could not to shoot him, the noise, there was so much noise…commands that just kept coming, telling me to kill Desmond Ashler. Over and over and over. I got towels for him and that plastic bag and then I hid in the closet."

Leon's voice was soft and calm. "Why did you hide in the closet, Jay?"

"The need to kill Desmond was growing stronger and stronger. I had to get away from him, but I didn't want to leave him alone in the room, I knew I needed to stay and protect him. If I stayed near him I was afraid I would kill him. The voice grew louder…kill him! Kill him! So I hid in the closet. I couldn't hear anything but the voices in my head, but I…I didn't want to leave my post, I didn't want to leave Desmond alone. But I had to hide…had to hide…had to…"

Leon took Jay by the shoulders. "Listen to me Agent Green. Listen to my voice. Can you hear me?"

Jay turned his head and stared into the eyes of the therapist. "Yes. I can hear you. Is Ciara alive? Tell me. Is she still alive?"

"Yes, and she's going to be fine. You didn't try to kill Ciara, or Desmond. You were trying to kill

Bradford. It was by sheer force of will you kept yourself from harming those you were in charge of. Firing on Ciara was an accident, Jay, *an accident.* Do you understand me?"

Jay Green continued to gaze into Leon's eyes. "I didn't mean to hurt her. I was trying to kill Bradford. I was trying to protect them from him. Yes, I remember."

Leon rang for the nurse. When she arrived he instructed her to give Jay a sedative that would allow him to sleep. Once he was out, Leon went into the hallway and called Neo. He told him what had just taken place and asked both Neo and Cayman to come to the hospital and meet with him and Desmond. They were already on their way and told Leon they would meet him in Ciara's room.

When the three men entered the room, Desmond looked exhausted. Leon was hopeful the news he was about to give him would help his state of mind.

"Desmond, I need to explain what happened with Agent Green."

Desmond sat up and picked up Ciara's hand. "We'll be right back."

"No. No, Desmond. I want to hear. Please. I need to know." Ciara's voice was thin and weak.

Desmond kissed her on the forehead and returned to his chair. He tore his eyes from Ciara and looked at Leon. "Go ahead."

Leon rehearsed to him the details of what Agent Green had revealed under hypnosis.

"So, you see Agent Green wasn't trying to hurt you. He was trying to prevent Bradford from entering your room at the hotel and killing you. He was trying to protect you. It was the mixture of the drug and the audio input that caused the hallucination, making him fire the way he did. He wasn't trying to fire through the door. He was trying to kill his hallucination."

Desmond sighed. "He must feel awful. I'll go talk to him tomorrow. I can't tell you how that helps me, and angers me at the same time. We have to catch this guy, and soon."

He turned to Ciara and studied her face for a moment. "What do you think?"

"I feel bad…for…Agent Green. Not…his…fault. So…sorry he…had to…go through…this. So…proud of…him."

Desmond smiled at her. She was amazing, so amazing.

"We're working very hard to get him, Desmond." Neo was standing at the end of Ciara's bed. "And we *will* get him. You can count on it."

Desmond nodded and turned his head. Ciara was already sleeping again. "I've been learning how to shoot better, been target practicing with an instructor. But I believe I'm going to leave the hunting and shooting to you gentlemen. I'm a doctor. I have no desire to be an agent."

"Please tell Ciara how sorry we are for this. I'll try to come back when she's awake. Neo touched Desmond's shoulder and Desmond stood, giving his friend a bear hug. "Thank you."

The three men left the room after saying goodbye and stood in the hallway speaking softly. Leon was shaking his head.

"What?" Cayman was curious.

"Oh, I guess I'm always surprised at what the human spirit can handle. The strength and resiliency just amazes me, and the forgiveness. But it doesn't just amaze me, it humbles me, and I think it makes me want to be a better doctor and a better human being."

Chapter Seven

"Have you gotten the encryption code?"

Bradford hated this voice. He was certain even his cell phone hated this voice.

"No, but I've made a good contact and things should go smoothly from here. Don't worry. I've got everything under control."

"Yes, surely. I've been watching your 'control' and I'm fairly certain you and I don't have the same definition of the word. I want that code. I've paid you a hefty down payment, in good faith, to get it. You assured me you'd have it. Time is running out, and if time runs out...I'm coming for you."

Bradford didn't like the tone of his voice. "I can easily return your money, don't forget that. This is *my* operation, and I'll handle it as I see fit."

"You try to return my money and you can kiss your life goodbye."

The line went dead and Bradford leaned back in his easy chair, thinking about options. This guy didn't scare him. Tristan Bradford could hide in plain sight and the man would never find him. Still, the lure of the dollar kept him thinking of ways to go about getting the algorithm out of Weston's head and into Bradford's bank account. He'd be counted as one of the richest men in the world with that much money in his account. What kind of prestige would that give him? The fact that no one could know he had it for several years was of little consequence. Eventually he would come out as the richest of the rich, and people would clamor to be his friend.

That line of thinking brought his mind to an abrupt halt at Neo Weston. Bradford didn't believe Weston was unable to remember the algorithm. Not for one minute. But if that was the case, what was keeping him from giving it away? If he'd thought that's what he'd planned to do with it in the first place, why hadn't he done it? What if he was telling the truth, what if he couldn't remember it, if it was lost forever? Was Bradford wasting his time and money chasing a ghost?

Maybe he'd sold the algorithm a bit too soon. What if he couldn't get the code out of Neo because it wasn't there? Bradford's buyer wouldn't believe that for a minute. There was only one alternative, he had to get Neo Weston. He had to make him want to talk. Threatening his family, his friends, nothing had worked. After the botched attack on Desmond, he should've come running with his mouth wide open spewing forth the code. But he didn't. Why?

There was no way Bradford was walking away from this alive without that algorithm in his hand. If Weston had it once, it was still in there, whether he knew it was or not. It appeared he needed a powwow with Emmett Matisse. There had to be a way to get to Neo without killing him in the process.

Bradford picked up his cell phone and dialed Michael McPheeters, a.k.a, Emmett Matisse.

"Hello. This is Michael."

"Matisse, it's Tristan. We need to meet. The usual place, six o'clock tonight."

"I'll be there."

The line went dead and Bradford put his phone back in his pocket. He had four hours to think about what he wanted to say and how he wanted to proceed. If he could only *think* of how he wanted to proceed. This op started out stained and was now filthy. He hated ops like this. In retrospect, he'd never worked one that had so many ways to go south and had done just that at every turn. He was exhausted by it and wished at this point he'd never found that buyer, and especially never taken the money.

Oh, but the money. How he loved looking at his bank account and seeing how many commas there were in that bottom line. It did something to him. It made his adrenaline soar, pumping the blood through his body at an amazing pace. He felt super human. He had to get the other half of the money and then he could relax. Then he could sit back and enjoy his spoils. If he'd let it, it could bother him how many bodies he'd had to walk over to get to this point. But why let that bother him now? It was over and done, and all the sadness and apologies in the world wouldn't bring those people back. He had only to take one more glance at that bottom line and those feelings dissipated. And to think there was almost double that yet to come.

Emmett arrived promptly at six and entered the cabin.

"Sit."

Emmett smiled. "You want me to roll over as well? Just watch me sit up."

"No. I want you to fetch."

Bradford chuckled and pulled out a chair for himself. He really loved this guy's sense of humor. He also appreciated his self-esteem. It was nice to not have people groveling for position all the time. It was plain Emmett couldn't care less about whether or not Bradford liked him. The money was singing to Emmett just as loudly as it was to Bradford, and Bradford liked that.

"We need to think of a way to kidnap Neo Weston."

"That's a pretty tall order. He's always got Cayman Richards with him, plus about three or four other agents at times. He's a walking fort, but I agree. He needs to be brought in for this to happen."

Bradford smiled inside. How easily he turned on his associates at the Bureau. He *really* liked this guy. He might make a great bodyguard when this is all over.

"What do you think would be the best way to grab him?"

"I think I should follow him for a few weeks. Figure out his schedule. Even if he tries to vary it to throw us off, he's always going to get up and go to work. He's going to walk from his car into the elevator in the parking garage every day at about the same time. He's got to eat lunch, though that's going to mean having bodyguards with him. I should be able to get a sense for bodyguard schedules and see where the vulnerabilities are. We won't know any of this without me tailing him."

"Yes, that's one idea. I like it. What else have you got?"

Emmett thought for a minute. "That's about it, short of killing his bodyguards, but knowing Weston like I do, if you manage to shoot one of his men, you'll be dead before the next shot leaves your gun."

"Why is that?"

"Because he's a genius sniper. He can *feel* where you are, *sense* it, and it only takes him a split second to find you and kill you. I've seen it. I know it's true. I should be dead right now, but when he shot me in the warehouse, Neo still had enough of the serum in his system that he wasn't quite up to his normal deadly self."

"Hmmm…I see your point."

Bradford rose and began pacing back and forth across the cabin, one arm folded across his arm, the other elbow resting on it as his finger rubbed his mouth. He did this for several minutes before stopping and returning to his chair.

"What if we convince one of his own to turn? Someone who's already turned and ready to go?"

Emmett's mind raced, wondering if they'd missed someone standing right in front of them. "Who?"

"Never mind, I'll take care of that."

The room was quiet as the two contemplated their opposite sides of the fence. Bradford thinking about how useful this additional source would be in getting the information out of Neo's head, Emmett reflecting on his concern that there was yet another leak at the Bureau.

Bradford was the first to break the reverie. "I'll make contact with my source. If I find out he's grown a conscience, you'll have to kill him. We can't allow our plan to be discovered. With my face on every telephone pole, it's becoming increasingly harder for me to go out. You go ahead and continue monitoring Neo. Keep me apprised.

Emmett nodded and grinned. "I hope this new contact works out the way you planned. I'll let you know if anything changes with Weston."

As he walked out of the cabin and through the brush to his car he couldn't help thinking something. *"Why haven't I ever gone into acting? I'm really good at it."*

Emmett chuckled to himself, got in his car, started the engine and headed back to his motel.

Chapter Eight

"Absolutely not." Cayman sat at his desk with his arms folded across his chest. Neo and Cayman had just returned from a meeting with the audio crew monitoring Bradford's cabin. An abduction of Neo was in the works with Bradford.

"Emmett managed to buy us some time to plan," explained Neo. "Cayman, you don't get to decide whether or not I'll be abducted. It's a fact. This is going to go down. We either plan the kidnapping on our terms or we're blindsided by it when it happens. I don't see what your problem is with the whole concept."

"Go look in the mirror, Neo, or maybe I could get a copy of your driver's license from, say, two years back, one with the name Justin Markham on it. Would that tell you why I'm against it?" Cayman was referring to the face and name change, both done by orders from the same man who wanted him kidnapped again. "It's too dangerous. We could put you in witness protection until this passes. If he can't find you, he can't take you. Neo, this man killed your entire *family*. He's not going to get his claws into you again."

"Don't you think that should be my call, Cayman?"

"Sure, why not. And while you're laying a plan to get yourself killed, what are you going to tell Sophia? You said no more secrets between the two of you. What do you think *she'll* have to say about your plan?"

Neo looked at the floor, suddenly aware of the one person he'd have to tell that would rather kill him herself than have him agree to a plan like this one. "I know it will be hard for her, Cayman, but what option do we have? Run from him the rest of our lives? Don't you see? This is our chance to meet him on our terms, not his. If he succeeds in kidnapping me on his own, he's calling the shots. If I agree to *allow* to be kidnapped, we have control of the situation. Doesn't that just make sense? And besides, Emmett and Leon will be there. I'll be fine. He won't kill me until he has the algorithm anyway."

Cayman picked up his office phone and dialed a number. "Grab the team members and come to the small conference room. We have something to discuss." He hung up the phone and motioned to Neo to follow him.

"I see what you're saying, Neo, I do. But I can't fathom why you would be willing to do this."

"I just told you, Cayman," he said walking beside him to the conference room. "For Sophia and me it's better than running or looking over our shoulders for the rest of our lives."

"We're *going* to get him, Neo. We don't need you to do this. We're very close to having all the evidence we need for a conviction. When we do, we swoop in and grab him."

They entered the conference room and sat down at the table. Neo studied his hands trying to figure out what else he could say that would make Cayman understand his position.

Andre Winston, Van Bingham and Preston Glenn joined Cayman and Neo in the conference room. Agent Jay Green was still on the mend from his experience at Desmond and Ciara's hotel room. The men seated themselves around the table and Cayman explained to them what Bradford was planning to do.

"What are your feelings on this, gentlemen?"

Andre Wilson spoke up first. His dark eyes were intense as he spoke. "It could be a really great idea. If we're prepared and have eyes on the target at all times, it could be something that might finally work in our favor." Andre's muscular build and medium height made him look stocky, but everyone knew his rigorous workout program and that what others might consider a little extra chub was actually muscle. Respected for the work he'd done with the Bureau, his vote usually carried a lot of weight.

Cayman surveyed the group. "Anyone else?"

"I'm not sure I agree," said Preston. "Assuming Neo is even willing to *agree* to something like this - "

"He is," interrupted Neo.

Preston continued, his blue eyes glancing quickly at Neo. "Then, I'd have to say it is your choice, Neo, but I would be wary of it. Of course, I trust Emmett, but what if he's being manipulated? We know Bradford is smart; he was one of us, NSA, anyway, but still..."

Cayman spoke up. "Yes, he was one of us, but we believe Emmett has gained his full confidence. Bradford even hacked into the prison system files and read up on the 'file' we'd placed there about Emmett. I don't think he'd have responded to Emmett if he didn't feel he could trust him. What about you, Van?"

Van Bingham was almost six feet tall with dark eyes and hair. A weight lifter, he was well built and a very good agent. Cayman only picked the best for his team.

"If Neo is up for it, I think it's a decent idea. I don't think it's a *great* idea, but if we're going to catch this guy, something is going to have to give to make that happen."

Cayman was leaned back in the chair, watching each person respond. He turned to Neo.

"Okay, Neo, you know how I feel about this. I don't like it, not one bit. But I see how you feel about it and I want you to go home tonight and talk to Sophia. See how she feels about it, if she's willing, we'll do it, but I'm not going to send you out there without her being on board. Everyone agree?"

Agent Wilson spoke up. "We don't usually have input from a spouse in an op, Cayman. Why are we doing that now?"

"This rogue operation has been very personal to Neo and his family. These people killed his parents and his brother. They changed Justin Markham to Neo Weston, against his will. They stole his memory and used his family's money to fund their rogue operation. We didn't know about Sophia when the whole thing was started, but they made her believe Justin was dead. It's been a long road for this family, and if we're going to put them in danger again, especially with her being pregnant, we have to give her a say in it. This is personal for the Westons, it's not like any other op."

The three agents nodded in agreement.

"So, Neo, what do you think?"

Neo leaned forward and placed his forearms on the table. "I know exactly what I'm getting into, and I know what I'm leaving behind. I can't keep looking over my shoulder, I can't continue fearing for the life of our family. I have to do something. The way it is right now, we've been powerless to stop him. With my wife and cook in the house, Bradford somehow made his way in and left a note on our bathroom mirror. He hurt no one, but he made his point. He could hurt anyone I care about any time he wants. But he doesn't want to do that. He wants me. He wants what I have in my head."

Neo paused, then continued. "I could just put the algorithm out there, release it to the public now and ruin his plan. But what would he do then? Would he be angry enough to lash out at my family? To come for us, even though the deal was dead? I don't know, and I don't want to know. I want him found and arrested. Even if I did that and he never came for me, I would always be looking over my shoulder, and I'm tired of doing that. I'll talk to Sophia tonight and let you know tomorrow morning."

The group was dismissed and Neo stood. Cayman was still sitting at the table. "Let's recap for a minute, Neo. What we need from Bradford is a confession. If you don't get a confession out of him, this whole abduction scenario would be for nothing. Are we clear on that?"

"Clear."

The one thing he couldn't say was what a valuable asset Neo was to the FBI, and losing that asset would have consequences, especially after having found him again. Cayman was well aware of that, but Neo's family had to take precedence over the needs of the FBI, and to Cayman, that was what made his safety paramount. They'd all been through enough at this point for the sake of the Bureau.

"I'm going to head home, Cayman. I'll talk to you tomorrow."

"I hope you're still in possession of all your important parts come tomorrow morning," he said, smiling weakly. "I know this isn't going to be an easy conversation to have."

"No, it's not. But we're going to have it."

***

Neo was welcomed home first by Patrick and Sam. They spoke briefly and when Neo came through the door, Sophia was curled up in her usual spot, but this time she wasn't reading. She was staring out the large picture windows watching the snow falling. Winter was here for the duration, and she always loved watching it snow. However, today, her mood was more pensive. He could see it in her face.

"Hey… You're home early." She rose from the sofa and greeted him with the usual kiss. Her hair hung loosely around her shoulders, framing her petite face perfectly. She was so beautiful, so smart, so intuitive. "You have news for me, I can tell."

Neo sighed. "I wouldn't really call it news, it's more a proposition, with consequences."

The smile disappeared from Sophia's face and she took his hand, leading him to the sofa. "Tell me."

Neo went through the whole story with her, told her all they'd talked about in the meeting only minutes before. The look on her face nearly killed him right there on the couch. How could he ask this of her? How could he even have thought this was a good idea? It seemed so perfect until he saw the sadness in her eyes, and the smile fade from her face.

The only life he'd ever wanted for this incredible woman was a life of happiness and joy. But it seemed like all they'd ever had was fear and devastation. Now he was telling her that he was willing going into the den of a very large snake, and the reality was, he may never come out of it.

"Emmett is in there, Sophia, and he's one of us. He'll be there with me the whole time. The rest of the team will be close by. I don't see how anything can go wrong with this plan, and when it's over, we'll be free of him once and for all. No more fear, no more always checking behind us. And you'll actually be able to go shopping, buy groceries, clothes, cars, whatever you want. We would actually be free in America, instead of prisoners here."

Sophia lifted his hand to her face. He'd not seen the tear from her eye trickle down, but now he felt it on his hand. His heart broke, that he was breaking her heart.

"Tristan Bradford has threatened every one I care about. But now, we have a new life to consider, Sophia. Would he take our child to make his point? If I release the algorithm to the public, would he retaliate and take our child anyway? I have to protect our baby, Sophia, and you, and Mrs. Barbosa. I have to keep you safe, all of you. You're all I have left in the world."

She laid his hand in her lap, staring at it and stroking it softly. "Am I the deciding vote?"

"No, no you're not, but to everyone involved, your vote is the one that carries the most weight."

Her words were nearly at a whisper, and Neo realized there was no noise coming from the kitchen. "What was the vote from the others on Cayman's team?"

"Three for, one against, one on the fence, Cayman and I included in that count."

"Cayman was the one against, right?" Sophia smiled, a small smile, filled with pain.

"Yes. Cayman was the only no." Neo sighed, a heavily burdened sigh.

"You're right, you know," said Sophia. "I know we'll never be rid of him unless you do this. It could take years to find him if you don't and we would always be afraid, especially for our baby."

Sophia gently stroked his face. "You're the best they've got. I know you'll be safe, I know you can take care of yourself. And you know, my love will be with you wherever you go."

Sophia stood and walked into the bedroom. Neo started to follow her.

"No, Mr. Neo, let her go," said Mrs. Barbosa, who was, by now, standing at the end of the sofa. "Mrs. Neo every bit as strong as you. She be okay, you be okay. We all be okay."

Somehow Neo knew she was right. They would all be okay.

***

When Neo met up with Cayman Sunday morning he explained Sophia's reaction.

"I know the *only* reason she agreed to this plan was to protect our child. She knows if Bradford doesn't get the algorithm from me, if I spill it to the public for no charge, he'll take revenge on me, or worse yet on our baby. We have no choice but to stop him, now, before this goes any further."

Cayman stared at his desk. The room was silent for a few moments before Cayman spoke.

"Okay, well, if we're going to do this, we're going to do it my way. Are we clear on that point?"

"Absolutely."

"Good. I'll call in the team. We have a kidnapping to plan."

In a few minutes the team, including Neo and Cayman, were once again in the conference room and the real work began.

They knew it was important to make Emmett look completely loyal to Bradford. It could work, if everyone did their part. Neither Cayman nor Neo were worried about that.

The team worked to piece together a plan that would be both safe for Neo and convincing to Bradford. Once the plan was completed, the details of the abduction were conveyed to Emmett via dead drop.

Emmett picked up the information at the dead drop and hurried back to the cabin for another meeting with Bradford.

"What's the word on Weston?"

"Every Monday he stops at the florist shop on his way home. The last two times he's gone in alone with Cayman waiting in the car. I'll be waiting at that florist shop tonight. I would imagine I'll have him here by six if the traffic isn't too bad."

"Just make sure we get him good and secured before he wakes up. That's one guy I don't want to wrestle with."

Chapter Nine

Desmond moved carefully to his car parked in the hotel parking garage. It was his first day back at work and Ciara warned him from her bed that he'd best not try to do too much. If he'd been totally honest with her, he would've told her he didn't think he'd make it past an hour. He was exhausted just getting to the car.

He opened the car door and slid into the driver's seat, placing his briefcase in the seat beside him. It was dark in the parking garage and his eyes had to adjust to the lower light. Before they did, he felt a gun placed to the back of his head and he froze.

"Don't turn around my friend, I *will* kill you."

"What do you want?"

The voice was light, menacingly playful. "Why, I want you to go to work, of course. You go even one mile per hour over the speed limit on your way there and you'll regret it."

Desmond started the car and backed slowly out of his parking stall. He could barely make out the figure in the backseat, but not enough to identify him. He was pretty sure he could guess who it was, however.

Once the car was in motion, the man began his instructions. "I want you to go into your little lab and bring me five vials of your serum…aw, make that ten as long as you're there. I'd hate to run out of serum and still need more. I promise I'll give back any vials I don't use. And bring me ten syringes."

"Why would I do that?"

"Because I have a very capable young man waiting outside your hotel ready to shoot an incendiary device into your hotel room. That beautiful lady of yours will cook in a fire before anyone could even get to her."

Whether he did or he didn't have a man outside their hotel was irrelevant. The threat was real and he knew he'd do exactly what was asked of him.

"You're not coming inside with me?"

"No, I'm afraid my face is just too well recognized at the NSA. You'll have to do this on your own. Oh, and you'll have five minutes. If anything happens, or if I don't see you in five minutes, Ciara dies."

Desmond was formulating a plan of his own, and it would save both Ciara and Neo. This was Bradford, and if he wanted the serum, it was definitely Neo he was after.

Working with the NSA lab, and even the FBI lab, Desmond always felt like he'd found his niche. He thoroughly enjoyed his work and felt like it was something that made a difference in the world. Making that difference was exactly what he'd wanted to do all his life. He'd been devastated when he learned of the 'difference' he'd made in his best friend's life. Somehow, he couldn't let this man harm his friend again. Neither could he allow him to harm Ciara.

Desmond parked in the NSA parking garage and started to exit the car.

"Just remember what I said. I've killed before, and I'm certainly not afraid to kill again."

Desmond nodded and said nothing. He left his briefcase in the car and proceeded into the building.

He approached his office, slid the key into the lock and opened the door.

Desmond had a door that led to a short back hallway into the lab. He went as quickly as he could through the door and down the hallway.

When Desmond entered the lab he put on his best face. He knew there'd be a lot of 'welcome homes' and there was nothing he could do about that. He feared getting any of his techs involved in this mess. He needed to make sure he was back out to the car in time.

"Hey! Desmond! It's good to have you back. How are you feeling?"

Several technicians came toward him and he slowly lifted his hands to keep them back. "I'm very good, but still a little unstable. I'm afraid I can't give you all the hugs you deserve for your hard work, I might tip over."

There were faint giggles from the room and Desmond continued. "I'll be doing a lot of work from my desk today, but I'll need some placebo serum samples. I'm afraid the order of the day is to sit, but I'll come and check on you before I go home. I'll only be working until noon."

"Okay," said a male tech standing closest to him. "Let me get those samples for you. Can I carry them to your office?"

"No, that won't be necessary," replied Desmond. "I can carry them. It gives me a little needed exercise."

The tech hurried to the refrigeration units and grabbed a tray of five samples.

"Get me that bigger tray, would you?" asked Desmond. "I'll take ten samples in case I need the extras and then I won't have to get up and come and get them."

"No problem," said the tech. He carried it to Desmond and carefully handed it to him. "Are you sure I can't carry that in for you?"

"Yes, I'm sure, but I really appreciate the offer. Like I said, better for me to get the exercise. Carrying something and walking seems like such a small thing, but it helps with my balance."

"Here you go then. Let us know if you need anything."

"Will do."

Desmond left the lab and closed the door behind him. There was a reason he took the placebo serums. If he did have to inject his friend, he knew Neo was smart enough to go along with the hoax and Bradford would be none the wiser. He walked around his desk and opened the top side drawer. He pulled out ten syringes and stuffed them in his jacket pocket. From under his desk he pulled out a transport bag, made especially for keeping small vials safe during transport.

He walked to his door and out into the hallway, carefully gripping the transport case. He needed to hurry, time was running out and he needed to get to his car. As he walked toward the exit, he heard a voice behind him.

"Hey Desmond! It's great to see you back in the groove of things." Mason Smithing, one of the office supervisors strode up to Desmond and shook his hand vigorously. Mason Smithing did everything vigorously.

"Thanks, Mason," said Desmond. "I was just heading back home again. I find getting here took about all my strength."

"Oh, here," he said, reaching for Desmond's arm. "Let me help you out."

Desmond feigned a chuckled and said, "Actually, Mason, I'm told I have to do these things by myself. But it's sure good to see you. I'll be back tomorrow. Let's get some lunch this week."

"Sounds good," replied Mason. "You gonna be okay on your own then?"

"Oh yes," said Desmond. "I move a little slow, but I get there."

"Okay, see you around."

Mason disappeared around the corner, and Desmond continued to his car. He opened the driver's side door and saw Bradford behind the steering wheel.

"You're on the other side for the trip home."

Desmond walked around the car and got into the front passenger seat. Immediately Desmond felt a sting to his neck and everything went black.

When he woke again, he was blindfolded and his arms were chained to a wall. He was sitting on the floor and listened intently to the voices around him, trying to get a feel for what they were after. Two men were arguing, one was Bradford, but he couldn't place the other voice.

"When did you decide to pull this stunt?" said the first voice.

"I don't report to you, Matisse. I'm running this op and you'll do what I say."

"How am I supposed to feel secure with the plan when you're not working the plan? You could so easily have been caught."

"Listen, you're the one who offered your services to *me*. I was doing fine on my own. If I feel like you need to know something, I'll make sure you're filled in. Otherwise, keep your mouth shut and do what you're told."

Desmond heard the name Matisse and knew it was Emmett. He'd heard about the prison break and now felt like there was no way he was going to get out of this alive. He tried to remain calm, hoping they'd think he hadn't come to yet.

The room was quiet for a few minutes.

"What do you plan to do with him?" Emmett's voice was angry.

"He's going to help me get the information I need from Weston. If that doesn't work, I have a backup plan."

Desmond heard the sound of chair legs moving across the floor.

"Where do you think you're going?" The voice belonged to Bradford.

"I'm going to go get something to eat and then I'm going to grab Weston."

"See that you're back here by six then."

Matisse scoffed and left without speaking.

The room was quiet. After a few minutes Desmond heard one side of a phone conversation.

"I'm getting the package tonight. I should have your product for you tomorrow, or the next day at the latest. I have yet to talk to the 'doctor' about how this will work, and if it doesn't work, I have another resource."

There was silence while the person on the other end of the phone call spoke.

"Yes, I know this is late. These things sometimes take longer than expected."

Another silence.

"Listen, I'm doing the best I can. I've told you before you don't need to worry - "

Desmond could hear a very angry voice but couldn't make out anything that was being said.

"I don't need your money, and I don't need your threats. I've got a long line of people waiting for this product. If you're going to threaten me, I also have a plan in place and you will go down the minute I go down. Trust me. Now back off or I'll wire you your down payment back and go with another buyer. You got that?"

The man had evidently calmed down because Desmond couldn't hear a response. Bradford ended the call without speaking again.

"Imbecile. Does he really think he'd control this operation? *I* control the op. I *always* control the op. I knew I should have gone with that second buyer."

The room went quiet and Desmond could hear the sound of feet pacing not far from him. He continued to keep still, hoping somehow someone knew where he was and would be there soon. But realistically, how could they?

Who was taking care of Ciara? She would be worried sick. She was awake and alert now, and he'd had a difficult time keeping her in bed. Fortunately a home health nurse stayed with her during the time planned for Desmond to be at work. He could only hope someone had the presence of mind to call Cayman or Neo. However, from the sounds of it, Neo was about to experience the same thing as Desmond had just experienced.

Chapter Ten

The Bureau plan was formulated, and all that remained was to put it in motion. It was late when Neo entered the penthouse that evening.

"Mrs. Neo very tired. She go to bed already."

"It's late, Mrs. Barbosa. You need your rest, too, you know. Sleep well."

"Mr. Neo is nice man. Yes, I go to bed, too."

Neo strode into the dark bedroom and removed his clothes without turning the light on. He crawled under the covers and felt the warmth of Sophia's body. He placed his arm around her and rested it on her continually growing belly just as the baby gave a good kick. Neo froze in place, hoping he would kick again, but her tummy remained quiet.

"She already loves you almost as much as I do," said Sophia, her voice gravelly from sleep.

"I'm so sorry, I didn't mean to wake you. I should have stayed on my side of the bed."

Sophia turned over and giggled. "You didn't wake me. Our daughter woke me with that enormous kick. She was just so excited to hear her daddy come to bed."

Neo found Sophia's face in the blackness of the room. She was soft, everywhere, and he loved caressing her skin. "You're an amazing woman, you know."

"Well, so are you."

In his best high falsetto voice he replied, "Thank you so much."

Sophia laughed, trying to keep her voice down, but unable to do so. "You know what I meant," she said in a half whisper, half laugh.

"Yes, Mrs. Weston," he said, still in the falsetto. "I believe I do."

"Will you stop? You're going to wake Mrs. Barbosa."

"News flash…I'm not the one laughing."

The two snuggled together. Sophia finally spoke.

"Do you remember that day at the Bureau when Mrs. Barbosa and I had to go into hiding again?"

"I'll never forget it."

"Do you remember your promise to me?"

"I think so, but refresh my memory."

"You said soon there would be no more tears. I know you have to do this, Neo, and I know you're doing it not only for me, but also for our baby. I know that. But I will tell you now, the same thing I told you then. Come back to me. Don't do anything stupid. Just come back to our family. We need you."

Neo kissed her and held her close. "I will. I promise."

He held Sophia until she fell back to sleep, then slowly and carefully got out of bed and went to the window. Snow was falling softly over the city.

There was something about snow…a reverence maybe. Car engines were muffled by it, voices as well, and the soft crunch of shoes and boots breaking the surface was a sound like no other. There was a certain amount of hushed comfort in each snowflake, almost a promise.

Tonight he would sleep next to his wife, and hope that in a couple days time he would be there again, safe and sound like he'd promised. He trusted his team implicitly, he trusted Emmett. He didn't, however, trust Bradford, and Bradford was the wild card in this whole hand they were dealing.

Sophia wouldn't know when the kidnapping would take place. She would only know when the guards at the door told her, and she'd be okay. As he listened to her breathing in the bed behind him, he realized the hardest part of this operation was leaving her yet again. He took great comfort in knowing Mrs. Barbosa would be with her. Sophia would need her strength, but he also knew Sophia was strong on her own. As Mrs. Barbosa said, "They would all be okay."

***

Neo kissed his wife goodbye that next morning and left the penthouse quickly, closing the door behind him. Best to tear the bandage off quickly.

"You take care of her for me," he said to the two Richards brothers. "Keep her safe. I'm counting on you."

Patrick laid his hand on Neo's shoulder. "We'll make sure she's safe. You just make sure *you* stay safe out there."

Neo nodded and strode to the elevator. The doors opened, he stepped inside and nodded again to the brothers as the doors closed.

The Monday went by as planned. It seemed like all the days ran together for the last month as there had been no weekends off, no eight-to-five for the most part. When Mrs. Barbosa complained too much, he made sure he was home for dinner, but he didn't get that luxury very often. This last weekend was no exception, and now, as the day went by he had to keep reminding himself what day it was. With the last of the prep completed, now it was time to execute the plan.

A call came into Cayman's cell phone while the team was reviewing the timeline and details of the abduction plan. As the call progressed, it was clear Cayman was receiving some unwanted information and the room fell silent.

"Get someone over to the hotel as soon as you can. Make sure the home health nurse stays with Ciara, she's going to need the support." Cayman hung up the phone and ran his hand through his hair.

"They took Desmond."

Neo was instantly angry. "When? Why didn't Emmett tell us this was part of the plan?"

"I'd be willing to bet Emmett didn't know. It makes sense Bradford would do this. He has to be the one in control."

"How long ago? From where?"

"It was this morning, from the NSA."

"Are they sure it was Bradford? How could he just stroll up to the NSA and grab Desmond? That doesn't seem possible."

"According to his med techs Desmond took a tray of ten vials of the placebo serum and said he was going to be doing some work in his office. When they went to check on him for lunch, he was gone. At first they figured he'd just gone home early. However, he never brought the vials back. Between the time the med techs contacted us and Desmond was reported missing, we got a report from the team listening in on the cabin telling us Desmond was at the cabin."

Cayman assembled the team and instructions were given.

"Today is abduction day. Desmond is now the wrench thrown into the day. We have no time to waste. You know this has to go down as realistically as possible in the off chance that Bradford is watching it. In order to make Emmett look good, we need everything to go as planned.

"Be on your toes. When the call comes in that Neo has been taken, follow the plan to the letter. If there are any issues, call me before making the change. Clear?"

All heads in the room nodded.

"Let's get his guy once and for all."

The team left the room and Neo checked the clock. "I need to be at the florist in twenty-five minutes. We'd best get moving."

Neo pulled up in front of the florist shop leaving Cayman in the car. Since the day they'd learned of Bradford's plan to abduct Neo, Cayman had accompanied Neo home each night. They needed it to look like part of the usual day's schedule. On this Monday, it was no different.

Neo entered the florist shop and ordered the flowers. The florist had been replaced with a female agent and any shoppers were tended to quickly, so by the time Neo entered the shop it was clear of all customers.

"How about lilies this time, Mr. Weston? I'm sure she'll love this bouquet."

While they talked back and forth, the rear door of the shop flew open and a black cartridge rolled into the main area of the shop. Neo nodded to the agent and she dropped down behind the counter. Neo pretended to run for the door, but allowed the gas to overtake him and the room faded to black.

Cayman kept up the pretense and when he saw the smoke through the glass door and windows of the shop, he quickly called for an ambulance. He jumped from the vehicle and opened the back of the SUV and pulled out a gas mask, put it on and rushed into the shop, pulling out the 'florist' who was knocked unconscious by the gas. He searched the shop for other customers, knowing no one would be there, and when his team pulled up he rushed outside and called to them to them check the back alley. No one was there and, as planned, Neo was gone.

***

Neo began to come around and heard Desmond's voice. He was glad to hear his friend was still alive.

"You can't use that serum yet." Desmond sounded frustrated.

"Why not? He's already out, it would be a good time to do it before he wakes up."

Neo could feel someone moving his arm. His panic level heightened, but he forced himself to remain still.

"Listen to me! If you use that before all the gas has left his body, it won't work the way you want it to. If he *has* remembered the code you want, putting that serum in him will make it disappear again. You *can't* use the serum on him yet."

Neo had a feeling Desmond was pushing for more time, but he had no way of knowing for sure. Whatever the intent, the result was that Bradford backed off.

Sitting on the floor, Neo could feel his hands cuffed over his head and attached to the wall. He opened his eyes slowly and saw Bradford sitting in front of him, watching him.

"Ah, he awakes."

Neo was surprised at how slurred his words were when he tried to respond, but he spoke anyway.

"What are you doing, Bradford? You're taking a huge risk doing this." Neo scanned the room and saw Emmett standing behind Bradford. "Ah, I see you're in good company. You seem to run with traitors of late and you've got a good one watching your back. That sounds like trouble."

His words were becoming clearer and clearer the more he spoke. Bradford stood and his fist hit Neo's jaw full on. Neo tasted blood.

"He always was a mouthy guy," smiled Emmett. "Most of us could hardly stand him."

Bradford stood and moved to Desmond, pulling his sidearm and placing the barrel on Desmond's temple.

"Mr. Weston, I need you to give me the algorithm that you've kept in your head. Are you willing to sacrifice your friend to keep it a secret?"

"You know as well as I do, if that bullet hits his head with the barrel that close it's going straight through and into mine. Then you're really sunk, yes?"

"Okay," smiled Bradford, moving the gun to Desmond's forehead, "how about this? Will that work?"

"Yup, that should work, but I can't help you. I've never been able to remember it, not even a piece of it. Ask Desmond. He's been trying to get it out of me for weeks."

"That true?" Bradford searched Desmond's face.

"Yes it's true, I told you that. I told you he couldn't remember the code."

"He's telling you the truth," said Neo, adjusting his hands in the cuffs and looking uncomfortable. "It's a vault up there," he said, smiling ingratiatingly and pointing to his head…which earned him another blow to the jaw.

Bradford stood and tossed his chair across the room. He turned to Emmett, his face a mask of rage. "Why would you use gas on him if it was going to make him useless to us? You're as big an idiot as the rest of them!"

"How was I supposed to know? Did *you* know that? No, you didn't! We're not doctors! What's the matter with you?"

Desmond thought Emmett was being awfully vocal with a very dangerous man, but it worked. Bradford calmed down and pulled out his phone. He went into the kitchen and waited for the caller to answer.

"Leon Kenning, my friend. How are you? I'll bet you're surprised to hear from me!"

Chapter Eleven

"Tristan? Tristan Bradford? Why are you calling me here? You're on the most wanted list." Leon figured Tristan thought he was part of the rogue team. He decided to play along. He hit the mute button on his cell phone and quickly dialed Cayman's cell using his office phone. He held the office receiver next to his cell phone, where Cayman could hear the conversation.

"Richards."

As soon as he heard Cayman's voice he took the cell off mute and continued his conversation. "I can't be involved with you, Tristan. I can't talk to you. No one here knows I was a part of that operation, and I don't want anyone to know.

"Yes, well, I can change that little oversight with a single phone call."

"Tristan, you can't do that to me. You can't."

"Oh, but I can, and I will. I need your help. Just help me out this one time and I swear I'll never bother you again."

"How do I know you'll hold to that?" Leon continued holding his office phone as close to the speaker of his cell phone as he could, hoping Cayman was getting all this.

"You don't," came the snide reply. "You're just going to have to trust me on this. You remember our friend, Neo Weston, yes?"

"Yes, I do."

"I have need of a good hypnotist, and since you're familiar with this gentleman's psyche, I immediately thought of you. Could you help me out?"

"If I do this, you'll leave me alone?"

"Yes." Bradford's voice was quite believable, but Leon knew full well he wouldn't do what he said.

"What is it you want from him?"

"I need the algorithm. I've got a buyer ready in the wings and he's getting a little pushy. I need to get the information out of Weston as quickly as I can. He says he can't remember, but I won't believe that until he's hypnotized and still can't remember it."

"Tell me where you are. I'll be there as soon as I can, but I'd better get tomorrow's appointments cancelled and reschedule, just in case this goes longer than you think it will."

Bradford gave Leon the address and coordinates for the cabin. "Use your secretary to make those changes. I'm feeling very magnanimous at this moment and I'll give you one hour to get here."

"Is this a good number to call you? I'll let you know when I'm almost there."

"Absolutely. I'll be waiting to hear from you."

The call ended and Leon put his office phone receiver to his ear. "He wants a meet. What do you want me to do? He obviously thinks I was part of the rogue op. I don't think the head communicated very well with the tail in this op."

"Doesn't sound like it, but we could sure use this. I'll need to know Desmond's condition when you get there. I'd like to put a camera on you, probably a button camera. Are you okay with that?"

"Whatever works, but it'll have to be fast. I only have an hour."

Cayman hurried back from the florist shop to help get Leon ready for his trip to the cabin. It took only a few minutes to get the camera set up and installed on Leon's shirt. Instead of the front of his shirt, which Bradford would know to look at, they placed it on Leon's cuff, installing the microphone just under his collar and out of sight. "I'm not going to give you an ear piece because Bradford might look for that. The cuff cameras are new enough I doubt he'll know to look for one. Now, you're going to have to work a little harder to get us what we need, but you can do it. Just act naturally and get the job done and get out of there. If they haven't found Neo's earpiece we'll be feeding him information from our end. We haven't received confirmation he's listening yet, could be because he's been knocked out."

After a quick audio and video check to make sure the equipment was working, Cayman put his hand on Leon's shoulder, trying not to show his concern. Leon wasn't a trained agent, and in a scenario such as this, there was so very much that could go wrong.

"You go, Leon. We'll tail you until we feel it's unsafe to go any further. We don't want to spook him, but we'll be close. If anything goes south, the helicopter and ground teams will be ready. We won't be able to communicate with you, we'll only hear what you say and what's being said in the room. If you feel an imminent threat, I want you to say, very clearly, 'Let's all stay calm.' When we hear that we'll immediately close in, otherwise we'll wait until we hear a confession. Clear?"

"Got it. 'Let's all stay calm.' I can remember that."

Leon went quickly to his car, put the coordinates into his onboard GPS and started down the road. He watched nervously behind him and saw Cayman's black SUV leave the parking garage. He felt a little less shaky, knowing Cayman and his team would be close by, but in an op this sketchy, there were many things that could change a plan in the blink of an eye. The abduction of Desmond was the perfect example.

No one considered that specific turn of events into the abduction plan and now that circumstance had to be added into an already full equation. What would he do if things did take a turn for the worst? He didn't know, and decided right at that moment he would leave the contingency planning to the guys who knew what to do. He checked his rearview mirror. The SUV was still behind him.

It took about thirty minutes to get to the cabin from the Hoover building. Leon dialed Bradford's number. "I'm about three minutes out."

"You made good time. I'll watch for you."

The call ended and Leon continued down the road and to the coordinates given him. He saw the cabin right away and pulled into the muddied drive, parked the car and said to the team, "I'm here and I'm going in." He exited his car and headed to the front door of the cabin. Emmett Matisse answered the door before Leon had a chance to knock. Leon tried to keep his voice calm.

"Well there you are, Emmett," he said grinning and holding out his hand to shake Emmett's. "I wondered where you got off to."

Emmett shook his hand, gently pulling him into the house, then stepped to the doorframe and quickly scanned the area for anyone who might have followed Leon's car. Satisfied no one had, he closed the door.

"Hey, Tristan. How've you been?" Leon shook his hand. "You've been a hard man to find. It's been entertaining watching the Bureau chase you."

Bradford nodded and chuckled. "I'd introduce you to my 'guests,' but I believe you've already met." Bradford waved his hand in the direction of Neo and Desmond. Desmond glared at Leon.

"Yes, yes, I believe I *do* know them." Leon raised his arm and rubbed his forehead, allowing the camera to capture the two prisoners. "You realize they can't be allowed to leave here. No one can know I was part of the op."

"No worries. We've got that covered. Now, to business… Can you do what I asked of you?"

"I can sure try," smiled Leon, "but I'm going to need everyone not being hypnotized out of the cabin. I'm sure you can see why. Any distraction will ruin the hypnotic suggestion. As for Mr. Ashler, here, have you got a sleep agent for him? Make it something light that will keep him out for a while. I'll need about forty-five minutes."

"No problem." Emmett leaned over Desmond and gave him a shot in the neck. "We figured you'd need something like that."

"Hypnotism to extract something so deeply buried can easily be ruined by distractions. If you stay you'll need to be completely quiet. If you have listening devices you can listen in from another room, or from your car. What do you two want to do?"

"I haven't had time to install any listening devices. We'll go out front and sit in the car. I trust you completely, Leon, and if this works, you'll be paid very well."

Emmett and Bradford went out the front door and Leon watched them get in the car already parked there when he arrived. He turned quickly to Neo.

"Tell Desmond I'm sorry for the knock out drug. Are you both okay?"

"We're fine. Desmond's worried about Ciara."

"Tell him we've got her taken care of. She's very frightened for Desmond, but we've assured her we have our best agents on this." Leon spoke quickly and in whispers. "How do you want to handle this? You want to give me an algorithm or do you want me to tell them I couldn't get it? If he thinks you aren't worth his time, he'll kill you both."

"I think he's planning on using Desmond's serum if you don't come through. Desmond being drugged might buy us a little more time. Does Cayman know you're here?"

"Oh, yeah. He sure does. He's just down the road with air and land teams ready."

"Okay, write this down."

Leon took out a piece of paper and wrote down exactly what Neo dictated to him, consisting of some words, some numbers in brackets and pieces that looked like a computer programming language. Leon couldn't make any sense of it.

"Now," continued Neo. "He's no mathematician, so he won't know if this is an algorithm or alphabet soup. He won't know how to use it, either. What you need to tell him is that I stopped in the middle, that this is only a portion of the code because I stopped mid-sentence and stuttered, or whatever it is you head types like to say."

"Head types? Nice. I'll do my best. It's a little too soon to have gotten the code from you, so we'll need to keep talking like this. Looks like another five should suffice. If you stopped suddenly it won't have to go for the full forty-five minutes. Good thing you're on the floor. They can't see you through the window and you don't look very hypnotized."

"You know," said Neo, "once Bradford thinks he's got the code, he'll kill Desmond and me and possibly even you. If you can't convince him you don't have the whole code, this could end very quickly."

"Yes, but if I can convince him I've got a partial code and he believes I'm making progress, he may have me try again, which will buy us more time."

"It's been about thirty minutes, I'll wave them in and give them the bad news."

Leon stood and opened the front door, motioning for Bradford and Emmett to return to the cabin. Bradford was the first one through the door with a greedy eagerness to his face that frightened even Leon.

"Let me see it. Give it to me."

"I need to tell you - "

"Just give me the code." Bradford's teeth were clenched and Leon didn't feel like it was a good thing to try to explain before the man saw what was

retrieved. Once he held the fake algorithm in his hand, Leon tried to explain.

"I'm afraid that's not the whole thing, at least I'm fairly certain it isn't."

"Fairly certain? What does that mean? *Fairly certain...*"

"It means under hypnosis he stopped in the middle, like he didn't finish what he was trying to say. He stuttered and moaned and that was all I could get. I don't think it's the whole algorithm."

"Well, how can I know? How do I test this?"

Leon shrugged his shoulders. "I have no idea. I'm not a mathematician, nor a computer programmer. To me, it looks like mass confusion."

"This has to work. It *has to.*"

"Somebody sounds a little desperate." Neo grinned from his place against the wall."

"You. Tell me what this means. Tell me how to use it." Bradford shoved the hand scrawled note in his face.

"That information is no longer part of what I know how to do, thanks to you and your monkeys. I'm afraid the only way you're going to know if that is a viable algorithm is find yourself a computer programmer and see what they tell you."

Bradford let out an angry scream and slapped Neo hard across the face, leaving his lip bleeding. Leon and Emmett stepped back as Bradford continued his rage. Tables were overturned, dishes thrown about the room. When there was no furniture left to destroy he rushed back to Neo and began kicking him in the ribs.

Leon and Emmett grabbed Bradford from behind, pulling him away from Neo. "Stop, Tristan! Stop!" yelled Leon. "If you kill him you'll never get the rest of the algorithm!" Bradford calmed down, breathing heavily and jerked himself out of their grasp. "Tristan, there is a small chance he could remember the whole string if I can be allowed to continue to coax the information out of him. It might wake up that part of him that's been moved to a corner of his brain he can't access."

Bradford, still breathing heavily, grabbed Leon's arm and dragged him into the kitchen, out of earshot of the prisoners. Whispering menacingly, he pointed his finger in Leon's face. "I've worked too hard to get this information. I had Raymond Mathens killed when he threatened to blackmail me, I had Justin Markham's family killed so I could use their money, and I personally killed three agents and put them in a car in a garage to make it look like suicide. You make this work, or you'll be as dead as they're going to be." He pointed to the two men in the other room.

That statement made Leon fairly certain he'd be staying at the cabin that night.

Chapter Twelve

Within seconds of the words leaving Bradford's mouth the sound of a chopper was heard overhead and teams of FBI agents filtered from the trees surrounding the area. When he heard the chopper Bradford's mouth dropped. He immediately pulled his gun, and staggering back, trying to aim with shaking hands.

"YOU!" he cried, pointing his gun at Leon "You brought them here!"

Emmett drew his gun with one fluid motion and aimed it at Bradford. "Shall we see who fires fastest? Yeah, he brought them here, but I helped. I'll admit it. I'm not what you think I am. Unlike you, I'm no traitor, and I'm no killer." With a shrug of his shoulders he added, "Well…unless someone *deserves* to die."

Bradford quickly changed the focus of his gun to Desmond. "Put your gun down or the doctor dies."

Desmond was slowly coming out of the drug they'd given him and stared at the gun barrel pointing at him.

Bradford wasn't looking at Neo, who moved his hand slightly to show Emmett his handcuffs were open. Emmett laid his gun on the floor and raised his hands in the air.

"Now," began Bradford, grabbing the man closest to him, "Mr. Kenning and I are going to go for a walk."

As he started for Leon, Neo quickly moved out from the wall enough to trip Bradford and he stumbled, catching himself. Neo jumped to his feet, but not before the gun went off hitting Emmett in the thigh. He let out a cry and fell to the ground holding the wound.

At the sound of a gunshot the teams outside rushed the cabin, forcing the door open. Splitting left and right, with Cayman in the center, several of the agents took position between Bradford and the prisoners. Neo came around one of the agents and stood in front of Bradford holding some very sore ribs.

"It's over, Bradford. You've made quite a mess of things, don't you think? And now you've gone and shot Emmett. He was just coming back from a gunshot wound. I guarantee that's going to make him *very* grumpy." Without taking his eyes from Bradford, Neo called to Emmett, "How you doin' Emmett?"

"Feeling grumpy," said Emmett with a grimace.

"Yeah, see? I told you. He's not happy right now, and he's dangerous when he's not happy."

Two agents stepped up behind Bradford and quickly relieved him of his firearm and placed him in handcuffs. He was frisked as his rights were read to him and led out to one of the SUVs.

A medical kit was retrieved from the helicopter and several agents were helping Emmett. Leon had grabbed a dishtowel from the stove handle when Emmett was shot and tied it over the wound on his leg. The agents were gingerly removing the towel and cutting open the leg of his pants.

As Bradford was being led out, Cayman turned to Neo. "I thought you'd grab that gun and shoot him yourself."

"It was a real temptation, but when I saw his face, he looked stupefied. One must never shoot another man when he's stupefied. It's a rule among snipers, you know."

Cayman shook his head and chuckled. "You are full of surprises, Neo. And surprise rules. I would never have known."

"Yeah, well, I like to keep you on your toes, Cayman. It's what I do, you know?"

One of the team was removing the cuffs from Desmond, who was still a little foggy from the drug. He was helped to his feet, still a little unsteady. The cabin was nearly empty and the paramedics were still working on Emmett.

"I have a question for anyone who can give me a straight answer."

Cayman turned and saw Desmond with his hands in his jeans pockets looking groggy and perturbed. "What? Did we not get here fast enough?"

"No, you were...you were ever so timely," he said, his voice dripping with sarcasm. "My question is, why, when some bad guy has a gun in his hand, and there are several *other* good guys to choose from, am I always the one he threatens to shoot?"

"Oh, right," scoffed Neo. "That would be *me*, not *you*."

"You can't be serious!" returned Desmond, exasperated. "How about when - "

"HEY!" A loud voice came from the archway between the kitchen and living room. It was Emmett, a large white gauze bandage was around his leg already soaked with blood. "I'm sure it's a small matter, but *I'm the one who got shot*, or did no one notice? Oh, and in case you were wondering, it hurts. It hurts a lot. And, for the record, this is the *second* time in this op that I've been shot. *The second time.* Now, if that's not some kind of record, I'll buy a round of beers for all of you. If it *is* some kind of record, I want a large surprise party with each of you in nurse's outfits. Not the pants things they wear today. I want a cute little dress on each of you with an apron and cap."

Leon, Desmond, Cayman and Neo burst into laughter.

"What's so funny? It's what I want and deserve."

Leon spoke first. "That's not a nurse's outfit you're describing, that's a maid's uniform."

Emmett's eyes took on a far off look as his mouth formed a satisfied smile. "Yeah, yeah…I guess it is."

The paramedics arrived, not a moment too soon, and Emmett was quickly and efficiently placed on the gurney and removed to the chopper.

"I think he's got bullet confusion," chuckled Leon.

"Oh, yes, and is that your professional diagnosis?" laughed Cayman.

"Yes, it is. It's a psychological term of my own making. I'll be famous someday, I'm sure of it."

The four men left the cabin as a CSI team arrived to clean the crime scene. Leon took Desmond to the hotel and dropped him off. Cayman and Neo rode back in the SUV. Arrangements were made for one of the agents to drive Emmett's car and leave it in the FBI parking garage.

"It's over, Neo. Done."

"I'm trying to wrap my head around that. There's this sick feeling in my stomach that took up residence there about two years ago. I think it's a permanent part of the stomach lining by now."

"I'd be willing to bet that won't last long. You've waited a long time to be free of these people. What will you do with the algorithm now?"

"I'm releasing it to the public. I want everyone to have it. That should end the issue of how much someone could make off of it. And it should also stop anyone who might still have any designs on stealing it again."

That night, Neo fell into Sophia's arms. Her kisses were warm; her soft skin against his was like a balm to the pain of the last two years. They were finally free, free to bring a child into the world, free to raise that child. They were free to live. *To live*, and to love without fear.

Epilogue

The two couples stood side by side as the sun set on the soft sands of a Hawaiian beach. The clouds were thin strands of orange light overhead, adding to the beauty of the moment. Leon and Rachel, Desmond and Ciara. Both couples decided since they'd been through the 'spin cycle' together, they wanted to share their special day. Cayman and Alexa, Neo and a very pregnant Sophia, sat in chairs along with other friends and family, barefoot and loving the feel of sand between their toes. It was a beautiful ceremony, one that would shine in their memories for a very, very long time.

Neo and Sophia came to the islands for a retreat three months prior to the wedding. They'd decided to have the baby in Hawaii, even if it meant staying longer if the baby was late. It didn't look like that was going to be a problem.

As the couples were leaving, the traditional birdseed seeing them off, there was a muffled cry from one of the crowd. Neo grabbed Sophia to keep her from falling to the ground.

"Sophia! What's wrong? Someone call an ambulance!" The panic in Neo's voice was uncharacteristic and made Sophia grin.

"I don't think we need an ambulance. We just need a delivery room. I'm certain we have plenty of time."

"A delivery room? Are you serious? Is it time? You have another two weeks yet. Cayman! Someone help me get her to the car."

Remembering how that same look of panic felt, Cayman smiled at Alexa. "I'll drive them, you bring their car and I'll meet you at the hospital."

"I love you, Cayman. We need to have another baby."

"You may be right. But how about we wait until the twins are, say, fifty?"

"Cute, really cute."

Cayman drove the couple to the hospital and, as planned, Alexa met him there. As the hours went by, sleep gradually overtook them and they slept in the hard plastic seats of the waiting area.

In the early hours of the next morning, Neo woke the couple and invited them into Sophia's room. Sophia lay in the hospital bed feeling satisfied and incredibly exhausted, holding the sleeping little boy beside her. She opened her eyes when Cayman and Alexa entered the room.

Alexa beamed down at Sophia and whispered, "He's so beautiful, and…so tiny. What have you named him?"

Sophia glowed as she smiled down at her son. "Jamison. Jamison Lee Weston, after Neo's father and younger brother."

Alexa smiled and patted Sophia's arm. "That's perfect."

"Congratulations," said Cayman to Neo, hugging him and clapping him on the back.

"Thanks." Neo couldn't wipe the grin off his face. He was so in love with his wife in this moment, and it seemed all that love spilled over onto the sleeping infant beside her. He thought he'd burst for sure. "Do you feel this way all the time? Every day? How do you function?"

Cayman smiled softly. "Oh, some of that wears off as they age. The diapers get fuller and smellier, they cry louder and often for nothing, and they make horrible messes when they eat. I'm thinking it's the love you feel this very moment that makes all of that okay somehow. That love never goes away, no, but somehow we muddle through the joy."

The End

Other books by JL Redington

Juvenile Series (8-13):

The Esme Chronicles:

A Cry Out of Time
Pirates of Shadowed Time
A View Through Time
A River In Time

Broken Heart Series:

The Lies That Save Us
Solitary Tears
Veiled Secrets
Softly She Leaves
Loves New Dawning

Passions in the Park:

Love Me Anyway
Cherish Me Always
Embrace Me Forever

Duty and Deception:
Novella Series

Erased
Entangled
Enlightened
Extracted
Eradicated

Come join me on
My Website: www.jlredington.com
Facebook: Author JL Redington
Email: contact@jlredington.com
Twitter: @jlredington

Made in the USA
Charleston, SC
02 July 2015